# ATTICUS

## CHARLES EDWIN

CHARLES EDWIN BOOKS

# CONTENTS

# ACKNOWLEDGEMENTS

**To my amazing wife**. Thank you for always being interested in my project. Whether you were asking how writing was going, how close to my own deadlines I was, and etc. Having you keep me focused really meant a lot to me. Even though I might've rolled my eyes at having to get back to it. Without you being in my corner and offering advice, listening to me prattle on about ideas, or even just complain about the process I may have not got anything done with any real speed. Thank you for hyping me up, sharing my posts, telling other people about what I'm doing, and just in general being excited. Thank you, my love! P.s. also sorry for hogging the TV for weeks while I played through different games for research.

**Elisabeth Garner**. You were my first *book* friend and ever since have always been behind the scenes hyping me up. Whether it was a bad mental health day, or just feeling like my writing was trash. I appreciate how many times you reminded me the opposite. You helped guide me through writing my first book and all that came with it. Whether it was showing me where to get ISBNs, beta reading, cover design, and formatting. You helped a lot with this, and I am eternally grateful for your help as a peer and a friend. Thanks for always being my digital desk mate!

**Mike.** We've been friends since we were kids. We grew up in the same neighborhood. You were the first person to support my patreon. You'd always pop into my 2$^{nd}$ job and ask me questions / demand for more chapters when I was working on projects. Those pop ups, demanding chapters, and DMs meant the world to me dude. I can't thank you enough for how much you've supported me, encouraged me, and pushed me to see my goals through. It especially meant a lot during poor mental health days and when I'd go hiatus for a while. Your friendship and support has meant the world to me and I may have never finished this project if I didn't always hear you in the back of head scolding *"When is the next chapter!?"* Love you dude!

**Scoom**. Thanks for always being you, man. You're never afraid to share your opinion regardless of how it might make me feel. And sometimes it really made me feel bad, hah! You always let me message at all times of day, let me bounce ideas off you, and are always so helpful. Even if at the time I don't see it that way. Thank you for being one of the first people to read Atticus and for sending me your thoughts on it. I hope you're continuing to push through you own projects and keep making video games! Thank you for being my first preorder and for being an amazing friend! Side bar, we should play smash soon!

**To the Betas**. Oh, my amazing beta readers! You were the first people who actually wanted to read my story! Some of you may not ever understand it, but it filled my heart with so much joy to know you wanted to do it! I loved that some of you commented your reactions or would DM me them as you went through. It was such a treat to read your thoughts and experiences. All your feedback really helped shape Atticus into its final form. My 1$^{st}$ draft ended at 35,000 words. After I took all your feedback and reviewed items, the book ended just shy of 45,000 words. So much of that is thanks to you! Your words of encouragement, feedback, reactions, and excitement helped this project see the light of day. Thank you again for your time and attention! You lot are the best!

**Gail**. You're my first editor! I just wanted to thank you for being so kind and patient with me. I had a lot of questions, and a lot of imposter syndrome while working through the edits. But you always left your DMs open. You talked me through things. Took time to help teach and educate me in areas I struggled, which were a lot. I just really appreciated the down to earth real talk. Thank you for being patient and kind, you're amazing, and I'm so grateful we had the chance to work together.

**To the Family**. This is a hard thanks to write, because I really didn't talk about this project much to anyone. Then when I started sharing it on social media you lot just popped in and went crazy with it. Whether it was preordering a copy, or in some cases more than one, sharing it to your own timelines, sending me messages, etc. I was really blown away. So, to Grandma A, Grandpa L, Grandma B, Grandpa H, Chris, Marea, Cori, Steve, Eric, Bobby, Kris (katie), Tim, Jon, and everyone else, THANK YOU!!

**Aunt Kathy**. This one, I think will be a bit of shock. But thank you for that fateful day when you overheard me talking to Uncle J about a story and saying "Is this a book? This story sounds amazing!" and then after I told you it was from a video game "Oh, that's too bad. I would've really liked to have read that. I'm not very good at video games." Since then that exchange has played on loop in my brain. It was one of the main reasons I decided to come back to writing. It helps remind me that there are people in the world who could end up missing out on some of these amazing and beautiful stories. Since then, I decided I can write stories like the ones that inspired and moved me. So, thank you Aunt K!

**Jennifer**. Thank you so much for always listening to me prattle on during down times. You've listened to this book idea, my next book idea, answered questions about kids and life. Thank you for always encouraging me and actively listening to my ramblings. Believe it or not, those little things can go a long with people. For me, it goes for miles. Thank you!!

**To the Tiktok / Instagram friends**. *What's good tiktok / Instagram fam?!* Oi, you lot are the bees' knees. Whether you're responding to my insta stories, commenting on whatever weirdo tiktok I made, or insta post I made. So many of you have helped me to feel seen, included, and valued. I had big issues with this when I was younger, and it was one of the trauma items that kept holding me back from returning to writing. All your kind words and encouragement really helped me get to the finish line. It takes a second to show kindness and it goes a long way. You lot are all proof of that. Keep supporting others and never stop chasing your dreams.

# FOREWARD

I think everyone is afraid to be vulnerable. Because of that we are always struggling to communicate with one another. Whether it's because of shame, embarrassment, or whatever else. It's easy to become lost in our own hearts. To end up as wayward shadows of who we were, or worse,who we *think* we should be.

Many times, in my life I felt as if I was lost in my own heart. Only to come face to face with versions of myself. Versions that were no longer relevant. Versions of who I thought I was. Versions of who I think I should be. I'd often find myself at war with myself and when I'd try to describe that to people, they just wouldn't understand.

To my friends, family, and readers. If you ever find yourself like this, then I wrote this story for you.

If you've never found yourself that way, then please listen closely to the words that are about to be presented to you.

I traversed to the deepest parts of my heart and back to create Atticus in hope that others who feel like I have might feel seen and heard. That they might read this and walk away not feeling as alone as I did.

Your words and actions have impact. Whether you see it or not. Every person wants to help, we all want to do good. It's easy to think we impact nothing and offer so little. The strongest tool of all lies within you. I hope by the end of this book you'll find yourself in a place where you begin exploring that power within you and start asking yourself what you can do.

## ???

The Doctor did his best to stay quiet, but his entire body shook with every beat of his heart and fear coursed through him as the walls of the closet suffocated him. His breath felt like a siren going off with each exhale and inhale. He covered his mouth and pinched his eyes shut, hoping it wouldn't find them. Its footsteps grew closer and closer. A deafening clicking came from outside the closet as the door handle began to turn and the door let out a long creak as it slowly opened. The creaking paused for what felt like an eternity before it smashed into the wall. Various pieces of wood pummeling the floor echoed from outside the closet.

*It is here!*

The Doctor's mind screamed, and his eyes shot open. Sweat fell from his face as he tried to remain calm and suppress every sound, every thought, hoping it would keep them safe. He looked to the boy sitting beside him. The boy didn't show an ounce of fear on his face, and he gently rested his hand on the Doctor's knee. His face was serious, and he gave the Doctor a nod acknowledging his fear. The warmth of his eyes eased the Doctor's mind helping to slow its intrusive thought. Their attention pulled back to the door in front of them as the sounds of wood creaking outside of their hiding space polluted their ears.

The floorboards let out a groan as it continued searching through the room.

The figure let out an irritated sigh when another crash came from outside the closet.

"COME OUT, COME OUT, WHEREVER YOU ARE!" It growled.

Despite the Doctor's racing heart, he and the boy remained silent.

"I KNOW YOU'RE IN HERE ATTICUS." Its low scratchy voice boomed as a loud screech followed.

"THIS TIME," its voice was abrasive "I'LL BE RID OF YOU FOR GOOD!" It finished in a roar, and they heard more wood splitting from outside the closet.

"HE CAN'T PROTECT YOU! THERE IS NOWHERE FOR YOU TO GO!" Its voice tore through the air beside the closet. Again, the sound of the figure's footsteps polluted the air. Thud after thud; creak after creak. With each step the Doctor's heart pounded harder, his body burning with the heat of fear and adrenaline. Through the cracks of the door, with what little light there was, they saw it. The nightmare. It had stopped its rampant destruction right in front of their hiding spot.

*It's found us.* The Doctor swallowed, emitting an audible gulp.

The thought had just echoed through the Doctor's mind when he heard a terroristic, joyful, chuckle from outside. His gaze pulled upward only to find a pulsing red eye sneering back at him through the cracks.

"FOUND YA."

# CHAPTER 1

A flash of lighting speared into the lake and thunder roared throughout the valley. Rain cascaded upon the manor. Visibility was just a few feet ahead thanks to how much rained down. The valley was hugged by tall hills and scattered atop those hills stood a sleeping and silent forest. Fields of tall grass and wild wheat grew atop the rolling hills. At the bottom of the hill was a modest sized lake, hugged by a sandy beach. From there a dirt path that stretched through and over a hill.

In the valley stood a large manor, home to a practitioner of medicines with a deep comprehension of the mind. The practitioner's name was Doctor Bram Finch. The man stood just shy of 6 feet tall with chestnut colored hair and deep brown eyes. He earned various degrees in psychology, medicine, and he also spent much of his time perfecting the art of herbalism. At this manor, his patients simply called him "Doctor".

His manor was a place for people to escape from the world. Here no one could dream of disturbing a resident, which made it the perfect home for people who needed help. Some had been placed here by order, people who were in deep need of mental assistance as they'd become a "danger" to themselves or others. Other patients chose to leave their lives behind to come here. They came seeking help from the Doctor to find themselves once again.

The Doctor stood under the awning of the kitchen doors listening to the tap and drum of the rain as it fell against the plants and decorative stones on the ground. The rain came so forcefully the sound drowned out all other noise. The Doctor found it was a peaceful melody that nature played for him. A cold breeze blew through, sending a chill up his spine. The doctor shoved his hands into his pockets for warmth as his breath hung in the air.

*It's getting colder.*

His body shivered as a chill came over him. The ranch doors beside him opened and out peeked the head of a woman. She had bright crystal blue eyes and wore her brown hair in a low ponytail.

"Good evening, Doctor," she called, her voice warm and inviting.

"Good evening, Sarah," he replied, giving her a smile as his gaze left the lake to meet her.

"Did you want to join me for something to eat? The patients have all eaten now and are off on their own."

"Gladly, it was beginning to be a bit cold out here anyhow," he said rubbing his hands together before crossing his arms as he turned to walk inside.

She gave him a smile and retreated inside.

The Doctor looked out at the lake once more. His eyes glossed over for a second as he slipped back into his thoughts. However, the aroma of oven baked chicken and mashed potatoes plucked him from his thoughts and back to reality. Giving his head a shake, he turned and walked inside shutting the storm behind him.

Across the valley, hidden in the tree, stood the silhouette of a person, it's gaze resolute and fixed. Even after the Doctor headed inside, it continued to watch. After some time, the figure turned and retreated back into the woods. The clouds lit up as lightning danced inside and the low rumble of thunder roared throughout the valley once more.

# CHAPTER 2

While the thunder had finally stopped, the rain continued without any signs of ending. Down the hall from the kitchen was a small sitting room. Inside was a little table that could comfortably seat one. Tall arching windows took up most of the wall standing about ten feet tall. Robust and heavy curtains were pulled into their metal hooked holders beside the windows. The heavy cloth was a deep purple and had golden ornate details along the edges and corners. Outside the windows was a garden housing a wide variety of colored flora. They were organized by size with the larger, almost bush like, flowers in the back to the tiny miniature sunflowers in the front. Off in the distance a river flowed from the woods and ran in the direction of the lake.

At the table sat a young woman. She stood about five foot seven with a welcoming expression, however, her eyes always looked empty. Her gaze fixed and unaware of his approach. It looked that her focus was somewhere else entirely, trapped behind a veil, and all that was able to escape to her eyes was sadness. Her auburn hair draped over her shoulder in the same ponytail she always wore it in. Her view fixated on the rain outside, while her book lay open and forgotten in her lap.

"Good morning, Abbey," greeted the Doctor as he walked into the room.

"Oh! G-good morning, Doctor," she replied, her voice shook with surprise as he broke her concentration.

"Did I startle you?"

"Oh, well, just a little," she replied in an awkward laugh. "I was just watching the rain."

The Doctor looked out towards the garden.

"Yes, it is quite beautiful," he stated gently.

Abbey gave a nod in agreement as her gaze turned outside.

"This is one of my favorite places to be, on a day such as this." He smiled. Hoping his tone would help her feel more at ease.

"Mine, too. It's so peaceful here."

"May I join you?" he asked before entering the room further.

The Doctor knew some of Abbey's past and before any engagement outside of pleasantries, he always made sure to ask for her permission. She had the power to welcome or deny his presence at any time. For Abbey, today was a good day. The rain helped with that.

"Of course." Her voice elevated and motioned to the chair across from her.

"Well, thank you," he said as he stepped into the room. Based on the exchange so far, the Doctor was hopeful about having a breakthrough today. He set his tumbler on the table, filled with his morning coffee, as well as a small, worn, green leather book he carried for patient notes.

"Are you open to having a session today?" he asked as he took his seat.

"Sure." Her voice rang with slight unease.

"Excellent." He raised his hand that was holding his pen with excitement. He opened his book and paged through it a bit as he laid his right leg over his left and reviewed his notes. Abbey was silent and continued to watch the rain. She started to fidget in her seat.

"How are you feeling today?"

"Good."

"Good, and how has your day been so far?"

"It's good too," she replied dully.

"Fantastic." he replied, smiling with his eyes. "What about today has made it good?"

"Um . . . oh! Ms. Sarah baked some homemade buns this morning and had fresh juice waiting for us for breakfast today." Her eyes glistened with excitement as she recalled her breakfast.

"She does make some wonderful, sweet rolls."

"Yes."

"What else?"

She paused for a moment, lost in her own thoughts. It had been a minute or so and she had yet to reply.

"Oh, well it's quiet today," she finally said, her eyes widening as she realized how long she'd been silent.

"Quiet today? Can you tell me more about that?" the Doctor asked as he tapped the end of the pen against his notebook.

The manor was usually quiet. Most often people wandered the property quietly. They'd spend time at the lake, or would be in session with the Doctor, while some took strolls through the garden or wandered about the woods. The patients were rather free in how they spent their time. Even scheduled meals were an open invitation.

"Yes," she said firmly with a small repeated nod.

"In what ways?"

"It's really loud outside most days. You can hear the river and the wind. It feels like they're always fighting for my attention. On hot days, the heat sticks to you like a wet blanket you can't get rid of, which to me makes everything more noticeably uncomfortable. And when Tristan and Davis are walking around, or playing outside, or whatever it is they do out in the fields. They like to run through all the grass and wheat which makes the worst possible noise as it all scrapes together."

His eyes widened at the statement.

*That comment feels odd. If I remember correctly, Abbey was from a larger city.*

The memory of their first session played through his mind.

*That's right. She mentioned the noise of the city bothered her. Why would the sound of just two people distress her so much? The difference between these two situations shouldn't even compare.*

He quickly scribbled down the thought.

She took a deep breath before she continued with her now rant.

"And don't even get me started at night. The night is meant to be a peaceful and quiet place, yet the frogs steal that away their insistent croaking and bellowing. I can never get any rest. It's very rude!" her voiced raised a few decibels as she finished.

"Abbey." He spoke softly, trying to gently bring her attention away from her distress.

"What?" she barked as she looked at him, her eyes narrowing.

"I brought you this." He placed one of Sarah's sweet buns on the table.

Abbey had been at the manor for a while now and he had come to know some of Abbey's triggers, such as noise. He also learned some of her calming conditions, such as her favorite foods.

*If you want to get on Abbey's good side, bring her food.* Her attention shifted from him to the pastry.

"Oh, a sweet bun, thank you," she squeaked happily reaching her hands out. Just, before she took it, her hands froze around it. "This is for me, right?"

"Yes, I brought this just for you," He reassured her as his eyes closed to smile.

Her face lit up with glee as she snatched the bun away, taking a large bit out of it.

"You're used to the sounds of the city, aren't you?" He scratched at his chin as he questioned her.

"Yeff," she replied, her words muffled from the large bite she took still filling her mouth.

"You've been here a few months now. How have you been adapting to life here?" He glanced up from his notebook, meeting her eyes, hoping to show her his genuine interest in her answer.

"Well, it is nice, and you are nice, of course." She gave him a smile, "I like mostly everyone . . . except for Rex." She glared down at the ground.

"Ahh right. Can you tell me what bothers you about Rex?" He was confident he knew that answer, but always prompted Abbey to explore her own feelings.

"He's extremely rude," she stated loudly, her grip tightened around the pastry squashing it in her palm.

"Your relationship with him hasn't improved?"

"No. I asked him to turn his music down the other night, but he told me to shove off." She lowered her voice mocking his comment. "And then he slammed his door in my face. If that wasn't rude enough, he had the audacity to play his music even louder!" She animated her story with her hands.

"Ahh, that would frustrate me as well," he replied with empathy.

*I don't blame her. Rex can be . . . well, saying 'a lot' wouldn't even be the start of it.* He let out a sigh as he recalled some of his own past encounters with the aggrieved teen.

"Yes, you get it! We have rules here, why can't he follow them!?" She was on the edge of her seat, pastry crushed in her hand.

"That's true. It's frustrating that he isn't being more considerate of your feelings."

"Yes, I don't like noise." She leaned back into her chair, poking at the now crushed bun in her hand and began to tear small pieces off it.

"The quiet helps you feel calm?"

"Yes."

"I wonder . . . " the Doctor said, as he drifted off in thought. He allowed silence to settle over their conversation, hoping it would encourage Abbey to further engage with the process.

"You wonder what?" she asked, her brow raised as she leaned forward focused only on him.

He met her gaze for a long moment before closing his book and tossing it on the table. He rose from his chair and turned to look out the window as he cupped his hands behind his back. He watched the rain fall on to the stone walkway that circled the garden.

". . . I wonder if for young Rex, if perhaps noise is calming to him."

"How could anyone find that much noise calming?" she scoffed in disbelief, crossing her arms as she turned her head quickly to look out the window.

"You find silence or white noise to be peaceful, right? The sound of a stream or the rustling of the leaves with a gentle breeze?"

"Yes, or silence. Both are very calming to me."

"And this too is calming, isn't it?" he asked, motioning to the rain outside.

She turned her gaze outside and took the rain in for a moment. They both listened to the orchestra the rain produced. The tapping from the roof above. The gentle tap of the rain colliding with the petals and grass from the garden.

"Yes." She nodded.

"To some this is nothing but a loud noise. Something to be scared of," he stated softly, the timbre of his voice low.

Abbey blinked as she looked at the sky.

"Did you know Rex hates the rain?"

"What, why?"

The Doctor gave a shrug to signify he wasn't sure, though he did, in fact, know the reason.

"Why do you dislike the sounds you described to me earlier?" he asked her, still looking outside.

She sat silently not answering his question. The sounds of the rain filled the room during her silence.

He left her to think alone for another moment before whispering to her.

"It helps to say what our troubles are, you know."

She turned her attention back to him. "But . . ."

"Memories are memories. If we don't give them words, don't give them shape, then they feel impossible to stand before. But if we can give them meaning with words, they take shape, and we can stand before them." He clasped his hands together as he spoke. He tried giving the idea of his lecture shape by using his hands. As she reflected on his words, and cupped her own hands, she let out a sigh as she released it and slipped back into her chair.

"I don't like it . . . because . . . that's where they left me." Her voice shook as she spoke of her painful memory.

"Who left you where?"

She swallowed hard; her hands fidgeted again.

"When my parents . . . left me . . . " her eyes swelled with tears as she was recalling her childhood. " . . . left me . . . at the lake." As her words finished, tears rolled down her cheeks.

The Doctor left the window and knelt beside her chair.

Through her quiet tears she spoke just soft enough to be a whisper. "I hate those sounds because they left me there. They left me alone at our lake and never came back for me. It was days before someone found me and I had nothing but the clothes I was wearing. I didn't know how to go home. I just wanted to go home!" She brought her knees up into the chair and buried her face into them as she hugged her legs to hide away from the memory as she sobbed into them.

Abbey turned to the Doctor, her voice bitter, and eyes red. "I'm not angry at them, you know? Maybe a little, because, well, it's a sucky thing to do to a kid" Her voice grew hoarse. "But it hurts . . . it hurts knowing they didn't want me . . . that I wasn't enough . . . " She turned her face back into her legs.

"I know, I know." He offered her his hand, letting her decide whether to take it or not. She looked back over to him after she heard him move and took his hand. Abbey sniffled and cleared her tears against her knee while holding back another set of tears.

"You came here looking to let go of that past so you could find your own strength to move forward, remember?" he said, his voice soft.

She nodded, her eyes full of tears waiting to be released again.

"Why do you think the others are here?"

"I don't know." Her voice was low and tired as she looked away again, resting her head against her knees.

"If you hate the sound of outside, because of this terrible thing that happened to you, do you think maybe Rex might hate silence because of something troubling him?" he asked.

This is what the Doctor was trying to work on with Abbey, the realization that others had their own problems. At some point Abbey had admitted to him that unless people agreed with her, then they were against her completely. She had made great strides in being able to talk about her past trauma. What it was, why it had such power over her, and she even started opening up to almost everyone here. Abbey was now at the point of the Doctor's process where she needed to begin learning to acknowledge that other's actions may not be because of her, but due to their own struggles and hardships. That people are not inherently out to get her.

"You think Rex's parents abandoned him somewhere quiet!" she questioned, her wrists pressing into her knees.

"I'm not sure." The Doctor gave a shrug "That's for Rex to know. But if that was the case, how would that make you feel?"

As her brow furrowed, she stared hard into the floor.

"Guilty. Really guilty," she replied, her voice low.

"Why?"

"I've been really impatient and angry towards him. But, if he's like me, then . . . " She started thinking about how Rex must feel like she does. " . . . oh no . . . " she whispered.

"No Abbey, you are not responsible for what's happened to Rex," he said as he shook his head.

"But am I any better for demanding that he live in a way that just appeases me?" Her voice growled at the idea.

"Your needs are valid Abbey."

"And so are his," she insisted slamming her hands against the table in protest.

"You're right." He nodded in agreement.

Her gaze shifted around the room from the Doctor to the floor, to the window. Her eyes scanned over things only she could see as she continued thinking about her exchanges with Rex, and what they may have really meant.

"Abbey, what are we thinking here?" he asked, hoping she'd be willing to share her ideas with him.

"I'm realizing that . . . or I think that . . . I should try to talk to him. I should try to think about why he makes the choices he makes." She nodded firmly as she looked him in the eyes. Her composure shifted from lost to resolved.

"Yes, I think that's a good idea."

Abbey was impulsive and while he didn't always encourage that behavior during her time here, this time he didn't get in her way.

"The next time I see Rex, I'm going to try and be more understanding with him," she declared proudly.

Her body language was energetic. Her eyes darted around, and a smile crept over her face. Her eyes widened as she looked at her hand discovering her sweet bun had been reduced to squished crumbs against the table, and so she quickly ate what was left.

"Well, very good. I think that's something everyone should do, too," he said as he stood up again, giving a stretch and picking his things up off the table. "Thank you for letting me visit with you today, Abbey."

Abbey waved her hand up quickly dismissing the Doctor as she mumbled to herself.

*Making plans it seems.* He softly chuckled as he saw himself out.

*Not all days are like this with the patients. For Abbey, today was a good day. All the right elements matched up for her to make it through these difficult conversations. She has started to get more familiar with finding her own strength. That is just part of the process in her case. Encouraging her and reminding her the manor is a safe space, that her feelings are valid, and she is heard when it comes to speaking about her past. They'll be most important for her growth to continue.*

He jotted down additional ideas as he walked down the hall and past the kitchen.

The two had worked hard on those elements. Today was huge for Abbey and the Doctor couldn't be more proud of what she accomplished with this session. A smile stretched across his face as he walked down the hallway back to the kitchen.

∞

Deep in the woods, up a trail, and through the hills stood a small wooden cottage. The inside was simple with a table, and four chairs. The room was efficient and to the point.

The figure strode inside, slamming the door behind it as it walked across the wooden floors to the table at the center room. It pulled out a small sheet of paper and set it down.

"Soon," the figure said as it turned to look out the window.

"We'll try again."

# CHAPTER 3

The sun hung high in the sky, its heat radiating off the grass deep in the valley. The Doctor gave his collar a tug as he let out a deep sigh.

*It sure is hot today.* He sighed.

Sweat slid down the side of his face and fell from his cheek to the ground. The Doctor was standing in the shade of the awning just outside the kitchen. With the clear day it was a great vantage point to take in. On the opposite end stood a dense forest that wrapped itself around the valley. As the hills rolled downwards fields of tall grass and wheat overtook most of the space. At its deepest was a calm lake. There Tristan and Davis played in the water. Their splashes carried up through the air from the lake.

Tristan's laugh was infectious and even though it was burning hot today, his carefree attitude and excitement brought a smile to the Doctor's face. He could faintly hear Abbey shouting to Tristan from the beach. Her voice filled with stress as cautioned Tristan not to go out to far.

*Heh, kids.* He chuckled.

*Even though they all came from such different backgrounds and experiences, they're able to make some kind of life happen here. I find that fantastical, especially given many of their circumstances.* He adjusted his tie again, the heat radiating from under his collar.

*Life will always happen. Whether you live it or not is up to you. I remember hearing that somewhere once. Looking at them really helps me to understand that on a deeper level.*

Having enough of the heat, the Doctor stepped inside. A blast of cool air welcoming him as he walked. He took to the fridge to pour himself some of Sara's homemade lemonade. After filling a cup with ice and drink, he walked over to the window to look out over the lake once more. The sides of the glass mug fogged up as its coldness clashed against the heat of his hands.

*What an interesting cast of characters we have here.* He took a sip. The cold liquid coated his throat and sent a refreshing chill throughout his body.

*Abbey, the woman struggling with abandonment and rejection.*

*Tristan, the child abandoned by his parents.*

*Davis, the young man who lost himself amidst the humdrum life of a business world now seeks to find himself again.*

*And then there is Rex.*

The Doctor took another gulp and fixed his gaze to the ceiling where a small fan slowly spun.

*Rex and Abbey's situations are not all that different in many ways. Even their personalities are comparable. Unfortunately, they both have completely opposite coping mechanisms, which leads to a lot of . . . trouble. I suppose that's what makes their interactions so explosive. Her parents abandoned Abbey near a lake, and it took days before she found help.*

*Rex's relatives sent him off to work for a few weeks but when he returned, they were gone. Since there was no note, and no word came for him, he stayed alone in that home for many weeks before officials found him. Even though he's a teenager, he's still just a kid. Officials found him to be irritable, stressed, and quick to aggravation. When one of the officials tried to take him to an orphanage he assaulted him, refusing to leave the house. So, the kingdom saw him as a threat to himself, and others and ended up sending him here.*

*If I can find a way for those two to bridge their differences, it could really help them move forward. But, Rex is a stubborn teenager, while Abbey is a young adult trying to recover from her own deep trauma, which causes her to regress to the days of her adolescence.*

He set the empty glass near the sink as his hands rested against the counter's cool stone texture. His eyes fixed on the three down at the lake.

*However, it is my duty to help them and help them I shall!* He clapped a fist into his open hand.

"Right, break time is over." He exclaimed with enthusiasm. If he could connect with these people, he believed he could save them all. He paused for a second as he realized this thought.

*Save them? From . . . what?* He tilted his head in thought.

*From themselves.*

A voice echoed around him.

The Doctor took a step back in surprise as he looked around the room.

"Who's there?" he called out he scanned the area.

There was no reply. After a moment the Doctor tightened his tie, cleared his throat, and pulled his notebook from his pocket. He scribbled down a note about the time and occurrence.

*Perhaps, I'm more tired than I thought? I should make sure to go to bed early tonight.* The Doctor finished writing as he wondered, then left the kitchen and made his way upstairs.

The second floor was the residence quarters. The Doctor didn't come up here very often, as this was a place just for the patients. It was a place where they could privately interact, get to know each other, or if they needed, a place to get away from others. Rex was one who regularly kept himself locked away, especially if Abbey was walking around. Most people stayed away from here during the day.

Rex was a teenaged boy who wore dark hoodies, jeans, sneakers, and often kept to himself. His dirty blonde hair laid loose just beyond his nose. He often chose to spend his days alone in his room. While at night he wandered the house and valley despite the warnings from the Doctor and Sarah.

As the doctor's feet stepped onto the landing of the second floor, he could already hear the loud aggressive music coming from Rex's room. As he had mentioned the other day to Abbey, loud music was a coping mechanism for Rex. He believed drowning out the world in melodies would ease his pain. Songs that spoke of what he would describe as his heart's true feelings. He'd often just lay in his bed, half reclined against the wall with his feet dangling off the side of his bed. Paging through comic books, fiddling with figures, or sketching in his notebooks.

Typically, all the bedroom doors on the second floor were painted white, but Rex had taken it upon himself to paint his door a deep crimson red with the words "DIE" written in black on the front in broad, thick, brush strokes. The Doctor could never blame Abbey for having reservations when it came to Rex, but the way they faced problems was just so different he was struggling with helping them find common ground.

The Doctor gave three knocks against the wooden door.

No reply came.

He tried a second time, but once again, no reply came.

"Rex?" he called out. "It's me. Do you mind if I come in?"

"I'm not here," a disgruntled voice let out.

"Then how are you talking to me?" the Doctor asked, shrugging and raising an eyebrow at the door.

The reply was delayed a moment and just as the Doctor opened his mouth Rex gave his reply.

"This is a recording." He said in a monotone robot-like voice.

"Rex . . . "

"Leave a message at the beep."

There was a long pause amidst the exchange as neither spoke.

"Re" He was cut off once more.

"BEEEEEEP!" A loud screechy vocal beep rang out from behind the door, somehow defeating the loudness of the music in that one moment.

" . . . Rex, I wanted to stop by today because I thought we could have a session. I brought some sodas with me, too."

No reply came.

"It has been a few days since any of us have seen you. Tristan and Davis were asking about you this morning. They wanted to invite you down to the lake today. Maybe you'd like to join them?"

He was met with silence, though Rex's music did turn down slightly.

"I could come with you if you'd like."

"Who else is there?" the *voicemail* asked.

"Abb . . . " but before he could finish Rex shouted.

"The voicemailbox is full. DON'T TRY AGAIN! BEEEEEEEEP!" A crash came from the other side of the door and his music polluted the air even louder than before.

The Doctor leaned in close to the door and tried to talk over the music.

"I'll just leave these sodas for you here. If you'd like them, they're yours. Otherwise, I'll come collect them tomorrow morning!" He tried to make his voice loud but also polite.

Of course, no reply came. He set the drinks down and left a small note to go with it.

*I'm always here to talk, whenever you want Rex. My door is always open.*

The Doctor then made his way back downstairs.

∽

Back at the cabin inside the woods the sheet of paper was still waiting on the table.

*If you're reading this, then it means you've finally found me.*

*But, you're too late. I've already gone to the manor. You thought you'd be rid of me after the last time, but I'm back. Either way, you won't be getting to Atticus. I'll keep him from you.*

# CHAPTER 4

The Doctor opened his eyes to darkness. He looked to his left and right only to see darkness. He turned around to more darkness. He continued to look out around him, in search of anything, but his eyes could find nothing but himself.

"Hello?" he called out. His voice echoed and faded into silence

He cupped his hands around his mouth, pulling a deep breath before booming again.

"Hello?" he shouted and was met with the echo once more before it faded into nothing.

He walked forward, or what felt like forward to him. His steps produced an otherworldly chime-like sound like shoes against crystal or glass. As far as he could tell, he was just walking in darkness and his steps were not taking him anywhere when suddenly, a simple wooden door appeared before him.

He looked around once more, but only the door was visible. There was no handle, just a simple door with an iron bar on the upper portion and lower portion binding the wood together. Thick cobblestones were stacked in an arch encasing the door. Examining all sides of the new door, the Doctor found nothing of interest neither on nor around it. He peered around it, not sure of what he hoped to see, finding nothing but more darkness. Giving a shrug he pushed the door open, a loud creak moaned from the hinges. As he stepped through, he found himself in a long stone hallway.

Wooden beams framed the stone walls while a dark maroon rug with ornate gold designs near the edging, ran down the hall disappearing into the darkness. Small sconces were dimly lit on the walls did not provide much in the way of light. A loud thud and click came from behind him. The Doctor jumped from the surprise and turned to no longer see a door, but instead a window. A confused expression stretched across his face as he furrowed his brow. He wanted to turn back and examine it further, however something inside him called him forward, urging his body to move on.

The rug ran down a curved staircase. The sconces provided very little light but across the room he could make out a small balcony with a matching curved staircase. As he made his way down the stairs, he could see that both curved down to a shared landing.

*Where am I? Is this a castle of some kind? I don't remember seeing anything like this in the valley . . . .* He made his way downwards.

The room bore the appearance of a grand castle for a king, or maybe a mansion of an infamous vampire. When he stepped onto the landing he looked to his right and noticed another short set of stairs, only three or four steps deep that stretched out into a large entry room. He continued to follow the rug down into the room while his eyes did their best to make out the rest of the room. Three large smooth stone pillars held up the balconies above and before him stood a large iron door. On either side of the door stood tall, stained glass windows, each showcasing a different image. Unfortunately, he was too far away to make out what the stained glass images portrayed with how poor the lighting was. On the east and west sides of the room, below the balconies, were tall wooden double doors similar to the one he had opened back in the dark void. On the walls were detailed frames each encasing a different picture of a person. In between each painting was a small sconce that dimly lit up the portraits. As the Doctor approached one of the paintings a voice rang through the air.

"Who are you supposed to be?" The words were harsh, gruff and gravely, the bass tone reverberated off the stone walls and throughout the room.

The Doctor jumped before turning in the direction of the voice. He hadn't thought anyone else was here. Scanning the room again in panic, his eyes stopped at the landing he had just come from. The landing that was once devoid of anything but the rug, now housed a large throne and on it sat a dark figure. It had dark brown, almost black, hair that obscured most of its face.

"Hello," the Doctor said his voice trembling. He did his best to steel himself as his body shook with fear.

"Come here," the figure's voice commanded, its tone filled with anger and irritation.

The Doctor swallowed hard around the lump in his throat, and he slowly walked forward. As he approached, he saw more of the figure. It had a cut across its right cheek. It wore a form fitting coat with a thick grey fur collar. Its arms were wrapped in cloth and its pants withdrew into shin high hiking boots. Every article of clothing was black.

He reached the foot of the stairs and stopped. The eyes of the figure pierced through him with cold contempt.

"I don't recognize you. Who are you?" it questioned, its chin resting in its palm and eyes narrowed as it examined the Doctor up and down once more.

"I am Doctor Finch," he replied, trying to make his voice sound more inviting than fearful.

"Doctor Finch?" An eyebrow raised at him as it repeated the name.

"Doctor Finch. Daaaaw-ck-tore Fin-ch. DOCK-tore F-iiiin-ch." The figure kept repeating this over and over playing with the intonations of the name. It's head looked upwards as it kept repeating this, as if it was searching for something that it just couldn't find.

It's head swiftly looked down again staring at the Doctor with an irritated expression.

"Nope, don't know ya," it blurted out abruptly.

"Oh, well . . . "

"And if I don't know ya, then you're not supposed TO BE HERE!" it roared as the figure slammed a fist into the arm of the throne. It reached behind the throne and suddenly thrust forward a massive scythe. The pole stretched towards the Doctor as the long-curved blade's tip only a few inches away from his throat.

"Who sent you here?" It demanded

"Sent me?" the Doctor questioned, fear and adrenaline causing both his voice and body to shake.

The figure let out a scream of anger towards the Doctor the volume causing him to wince in pain.

"Don't play stupid with me! *He* sent you, didn't he!" It screamed as its voice growled again.

The Doctor threw his hands in front of him, shaking his head.

"I don't have any idea of what you're talking about!" He pleaded. "Truly! I just happened to end up in this place. I don't even know where this is! Honest!"

"I don't buy it!" Its voice roared with gravel once again. It rose from the throne and gripped the pole with its other hand.

"And I won't wait around to see what you're here for!" It said loudly. It drew back the blade, ready to strike when a loud crash came from behind the Doctor. Both of their attentions snapped to the door that was now wide open. A bright blinding light flooded into the room causing the Doctor to raise a hand to shield his eyes. The figure hissed, gritting its teeth, in pain as it stumbled briefly, raising its own hand to block the light.

"I knew it!" It roared in pain and anger.

*Come with me Doctor Finch, hurry!*

The voice that called out was gentle and warm, and without waiting the Doctor turned and ran towards the light. As he ran from the figure threatening him, he noticed a different figure standing in the doorway. The silhouette extended a hand towards the Doctor. Behind him he heard the grumbling of the enraged figure. The Doctor looked over his shoulder as he kept running only to see two blood red eyes staring back at him as it started to give chase, and it wasn't too far behind.

"YOU WON'T GET AWAY FROM ME THIS TIME!" It screamed as it tightly gripped the scythe in its hands ready to swing the second it was in range.

The Doctor turned back to see that he had made it to the door of light and embraced the silhouette's hand. The hand pulled him through the doorway and as the Doctor looked back towards the pursuing figure the entire castle was swallowed in light. The Doctor did a double take only to see the doorway to the mansion quickly fading into the horizon, but the two pulsing red eyes still stared back at the pair. Despite the growing distance he felt the beings malice surging in the air around them. It's fixated on him.

"ATTICUS!" It screamed as they started to fade into the distance. Before the Doctor could find relief in his escape, he saw the large scythe swirling up end over end right towards them. He jerked his hands up to protect himself and closed his eyes tightly waiting for impact.

Then the Doctor heard a crash. He opened his eyes to find himself in his bedroom. He panted, absorbing his surroundings and trying to calm himself as his heart continued to race. He thought of nothing for a short time as his labored breaths continued. He looked to his bedside to see that his lamp lay broken on the floor and beside it was his pillow. The heat faded from his head and regained control of his breaths.

"It was just a dream," he sighed in relief.

Swinging his feet out from under the sheets he planted them on the floor. Rising out of bed, he bent down to clean up the mess. Only the bulb had broken. He removed the broken bulb and returned the lamp to the night table.

"I think I need a breath of fresh air," he said, arms stretching above him. He walked across the room, opened the curtains, and pushed open the window. A cool, soft breeze rolled into the room, pushing his hair to the side. He closed his eyes and took another deep breath in. The cool wind washing over his skin was just what he needed.

*The breeze feels good.* He released a breath.

*But, what was that? It felt so real.* He knew it was just a dream, a nightmare, but it left his body in shock and the fear he experienced felt real. It was like nothing he had ever felt in his life.

*I suppose either way, a dream is just a dream.* As he finished this thought, he opened his eyes and gazed out the window once more. When he did something far off in the distance, on the other side of the lake, caught his attention. Two pulsing blood red eyes stared back at him.

*"FOUND YA!"*

The voice rang throughout his mind and took him by such surprise that he fell backwards into the bedroom landing with a hard thud against the wooden floor. His heart threatened to leap out of his chest at any second and sweat formed at his brow once more. He clenched the collar of his pajamas and rose to his feet. Reaching up he grasped the window frame to hoist himself back to his feet and peered out the window again.

This time, there was nothing there to meet him aside from the light of the moon. On the horizon the dark silhouetted trees rustled on and the water of the lake lapped against the shoreline. His eyes were fixed onto the horizon as he tried to locate those red eyes once more. Despite the repeated attempts, he found nothing.

*That nightmare must be hitting me harder than I thought it was. I think I'll make some tea and put myself back to bed. Perhaps tomorrow I'll take the day off.* Clenching his collar, he left the room.

∽

The door to the cottage flew open and crashed into the wall. The glass of the door shattered spraying shards throughout the room. Hard steps came into the cottage. The figure looked around, only to find the cottage empty. Seeing a note left on the table, the figure approached. It picked up the paper reading what was left. As it finished, it crushed the paper it's fist and tossed it aside.

"Damnit," the figure said before it stomped out of the cottage and back into the woods.

# CHAPTER 5

A few days had come and gone since *that* nightmare had occurred. Meanwhile, life at the manor had been as it should. Patients lived their days peacefully and having sessions with the Doctor. It approached late summer, and the air had started to cool, especially once dusk arrived. Nothing strange had happened in the valley. Even with that being the case the Doctor was still slightly on edge, the memories of that nightmare sneaking back into his mind throughout the day. Even though he could not put his finger on it, in his heart, he felt something was off in the valley. That something more sinister was in play and his patients were no longer the only ones here.

The Doctor made his rounds throughout the grounds.

He shared pleasantries with Abbey while she was reading in the library near the garden. Continuing, he passed by Davis and Tristan playing down by the lake.

His ears were assaulted once more by Rex's music as it polluted the air outside his room.

Lastly, he returned to the kitchen to find Sarah cleaning up from lunch.

"Good afternoon, Doctor," she greeted him warmly with a smile and her hands were submerged in a sink of soapy water.

"Good afternoon, Sarah. How are you today?"

"Oh, I'm doing all right, sir. Just cleaning up."

"What are the plans for dinner?"

"I was thinking we could make curry," she said using her inner elbow to wipe away sweat from her face.

"That would be wonderful." His voice rose in excitement.

*My favorite*. His face beamed as he smiled.

"I can hear the excitement in your voice," she teased.

The Doctor gave a slight blush.

"Hah, you caught me." He chuckled.

"I'll make sure to make a little extra so you can help yourself if you get hungry again later."

His face lit up as a smile formed.

"You're the best," he exclaimed when a loud finger snap rang through his head causing him to wince from the pain. He grasped his head as he bent over.

When he opened them again, he found himself standing in a space that was completely white. Looking around only to find nothing.

*This feels like the dark void I found myself in earlier, only clearly the opposite now.*

"Hello?" he called out, his words echoing into the distance.

*Hello, Doctor.*

A gentle voice called back to him.

"Where am I?"

*Where you've always been.*

He cocked his head at the reply, thinking for a moment.

"This isn't the valley though."

*Isn't it?*

He stood silent for a moment in disbelief, scoffing at the claim.

*Obviously not.* He looked around once more trying to find anything that would warrant the voice's comment.

*Though . . . I might not be able to see any discerning fact that would support this notice, it certainly feels like the valley.*

He looked around a little more, taking notice of the image below him. While he stood firm in place as if standing on the ground, he soon realized it wasn't ground at all. When he looked below his feet, he realized he stood in the sky far above the valley, clouds rolling by underneath him.

"I'm above the valley," he declared in surprise.

*That's right.*

"But why am I here? Who are you?"

*You don't remember me?*

"No."

*How would I?*

*Maybe this will help you.*

The Doctor heard a low humming sound that came from behind him. He turned around to see the silhouetted figure from the nightmare. The one who burst through the front doors flooding the room in light.

"You're the figure from my dream," he gasped, pointing at the figure.

The silhouette gave a nod.

"Why am I here?" he asked again.

The figure gave a puzzled gesture towards the Doctor.

> *I supposed you wouldn't remember that either would you?*
> *Hmm . . . perhaps I've left you alone for too long.*

"What?"

> *I thought I had left you with at least that.*
> *You've forgotten your true purpose it seems.*

"What are you saying?"

> *You were brought here for a reason, Doctor.*
> *You were made for a reason.*
> *And it seems you've forgotten your true purpose.*

> *Your calling in life.*

"You're not making any sense," he spoke back. His heart raced as the words sank in.

*Why am I so frazzled by these words?'You were made for a reason. You've forgotten your true purpose.' Why does that bother me so?*

"What's my true purpose?" he asked.

People appeared all around them. Some were walking. Some were running. Children laughed while running past them in a game of tag. The air was filled with distorted sounds and echoing voices.

*Mommy, come play with me!*

*Wow, you're fast!*

*Yes, I'll get the job done.*

*Who are you looking for?*

*Why did they leave me alone here?*

*I can help!*

*Your curry is the best, Mommy!*

*Daddy?*

*I'm not a monster!*

*Don't leave me!*

*Where are you, Mommy? Where did you go?*

*I'm all alone now . . .*

*Why didn't they want me?*

*What's wrong with me . . . ?*

A bright flash blinded the Doctor and all the figures vanished, except one. When he opened his eyes again floating before him was a sleeping Tristan arms crossed across his chest.

"This is . . . "

*The one you call Tristan.*

"Right."

*Who is Tristan?*

"What do you mean?"

*Tell me what you know of the boy.*

"Tristan is one of my earliest patients. His parents brought him here."

*Why did they bring him here?*

"Because he has troubles with other people. He's overly shy and won't open up to anyone."

Though that was the answer that lived in his mind, it somehow felt wrong.

*Ah, your heart knows better though.*
*It knows this reason is a lie.*

*The voice is right, but why did I say that then?*

*Why was he brought here?*

He tried to recall why, but the memory was just out of reach.

"I . . . can't remember," the Doctor said quietly.

*As I feared.*

*Then allow me to help you remember.*

Tristan's sleeping body let out a bright light, and the sound of crashing waves came into the Doctor's ears. Tristan's body was replaced with a dining room, but the colors were in black and white. There sat Tristan smiling with a plate of food before him. Behind him stood two adults with serious looks on their faces.

"What is this?" the Doctor asked.

*Step into the room.*

The Doctor did as the voice instructed. As he entered the room the scene came to life and began to play.

"Your curry is the best, Mommy!"

"I'm glad you like it."

" I could eat this forever!"

*Tristan set upon eating the curry before him. Behind him on the other side of the kitchen sat his mother and father whispering to one another*

"What are we going to do about him?" the mother asked.

"I don't know. 'e's a freak," his father replied.

"Don't say that," his mother barked back under her breath.

"'e is though! You saw what 'e could do, that ain't normal."

She bit her lip, but knew he was right.

"Well, what do we do?" she asked again.

"We need tuh get rid of 'im." he said firmly.

"And how do we do that?"

"I'll fink of something. And once 'e's gone, we can get our lives back, yeah?" the man said with a smile.

She forced a smile back at him, but her jaw clenched at the uncertainty.

"Oh, Mommy! What are you and Daddy talking about?" Tristan asked.

"Nothing dear," called back the mother, motioning for the father to keep quiet and she walked back to her son sitting beside him.

Light filled the Doctor's eyes as the scene ended and he was returned to the figure.

"His parents wanted to get rid of him."

*Yes.*

"But why?" his voice desperate for the truth.

Another light filled the space before the Doctor and when it faded another black and white scene was there. This time it showed Tristan facing a lake. Without waiting for, he entered the scene, and once again, it began to play.

"Look how pretty the water is, Mommy!"

"Y-yes," she replied.

Silence filled the air as the tension rose.

"Oh, sweetie, I forgot something for our picnic today. I'll go get it quick," her voice fluttering as she lied to her son, turning to walk away.

Tristan did not reply.

"Tristan?" she called back to him.

He turned to her, giving her the same large smile, he always did. Only, his eyes were different. They weren't the big brown eyes she loved so much. Instead, they flicked and shined with an emerald green. She let out a gasp, she knew what this was. He was doing it again. Tristan blinked, his eyes returning to their brown color and his smile faded from his face.

"You're going to leave me now, aren't you, Mommy?" he asked as he looked down to the ground.

"N-no. I would never. I just forgot what we needed for our picnic is all." Her voice shook at the boy's accusation.

He slowly walked towards his mother and looked into her eyes, his brimming with tears.

"Let's go home, Mommy. I don't want you to leave me here all alone." He tried to embrace her hand in his.

She recoiled away from him as soon as his fingers touched her. She paused for a moment as she gazed into his sad eyes. She slowly reached down to grab it.

"O-o-kay. Let's go home t-together." She swallowed hard.

His eyes flicked again with the same emerald, green hue they had before and when it faded his smile returned and his tears were gone.

"Yay, I'm glad you changed your mind, Mommy." He lead her back to their cart, his smile stretching ear to ear.

Light took over his vision again and he was returned to the figure.

"His mother tried to abandon him?" he asked.

The figure nodded.

"Why?"

The figure didn't reply.

"Was it because of his eyes? What was he doing?"

The figure still didn't reply.

"Was it some kind of ability? And if so, what was it?"

*What do you think they are?*

*It was like the boy knew what was coming before it actually came. Could he see the future?*

"Can he see the future?" he asked the figure.

*An understandable theory.*
*And not without merit.*
*In a way I suppose he can see 'a' future,*
*but that's not really it either.*

"So, he can see moments in time before they happen? I've heard of this before. He has . . . oh what was it . . . Foresight?" the Doctor exclaimed, hitting his fist into his hand as he came to the conclusion.

The figure nodded.

*Yes.*
*The boy has the ability of Foresight.*
*The ability to see an event before it happens.*

"Why did his parents fear this ability? It's a gift, isn't it?"

*It was a gift.*
*However, humans are fickle creatures.*

"What happened?"

*They tried to profit off his ability.*
*Thinking they could let him tell people's fortunes.*
*But as is often the case with children*
*he had no way to control his Foresight.*
*To his parents it was only a bad omen*
*as every time he saw something*
*it was before something terrible would transpire.*
*A family member's death.*
*A robbery.*
*An accident.*
*Father losing his job.*
*Mother breaking her arm.*
*They soon began to hate their son.*

"They didn't see it as a gift to prepare for what's coming?"

The figure shook its head.

"And that's why he was brought here." The Doctor scoffed at the notion.

*Yes.*

*His parents abandoned him here.*
*Or so they tried to do.*
*Many times.*
*Until they were one day successful*
*but not in the way they planned.*

"What do you mean?"

The figure shook its head.

> *This will have to be the end for today.*
> *I am growing tired from this lengthy discussion.*
> *We shall meet again, Doctor.*
> *In the meantime I have a request.*
> *Remember your true purpose for being here, in this place.*

"How do you mean?" he asked.

The figure waved its hand and before the Doctor appeared all the patients of the manor.

Tristan – Davis – Abbey – Rex – Sarah – all floated, sleeplike, before him.

"The patients?"

> *Speak to them.*
> *Listen to them.*
> *Remember who they are.*
> *Piece them back together Doctor.*
>
> *And remember who you are.*

The area was engulfed by light. It was a moment before he opened his eyes again, and in this small respite he thought over the events that just happened.

*Who was that figure? Why did it save me before, what does it mean by what it says?*

*'The reason you were made, why does this cling to me so deeply?* His mind kept trying to piece together this puzzle.

His eyes finally opened and he found himself back in the kitchen with Sarah.

"My goodness, Doctor, you're quite excited today. You're usually so reserved. Has something happened?" she asked.

The Doctor took a moment to reply. He looked around, realizing he'd been returned to his conversation. It was like he was plucked out of the world and returned to the exact moment in time from when he had left.

*She's right, why did a boy-like joy rush over me at the mere mention of curry?*

"Oh, I'm just very much looking forward to dinner is all. But, I've just remembered something. If you'll excuse me," he said, giving a slight bow of his head and left the room. His look became stern as he pondered over the events that just happened.

*The patients seem to have the answers about my true purpose. But why was Sarah shown as well? She's my assistant, right?*

༄

The dark figure continued deep into the woods until it came upon a cave. It let out a heavy sigh as it entered.

"The kid isn't there anymore," the figure growled.

"It's fine," replied another figure. "He has likely reached out to him already. We needn't do more than simply watch for now."

"Sitting around isn't exactly my style. Why don't we just run in there and take what we've come for?" the first figure suggested with excitement in his words.

"Always playing the fool, aren't you? No. We will wait until the moment is right. We don't need all three of them knowing we're out here. Only he knows currently and that could be good for us in the long run," the second, calmer figure stated.

# CHAPTER 6

The Doctor spent the night gathering up materials and reviewing the journals he had made regarding each of the patients. He hoped that by reviewing each personal record he could find meaning behind the encounters he had with the figure in the sky. In different piles he compiled each patient's logs and observations as well as their original reason for coming to the valley.

☙

Patient: Tristan
Age: 6
Gender: Male
Likes: Curry, the lake, Fun
Dislikes: Solitude, Arguments
Reason for Visiting:
~~Needs help overcoming shyness~~
Abandoned by parents

Notes:
Tristan was brought here because his parents claimed that he suffered from extreme shyness and social anxiety that resulted in him not being able to make friends with other children. However, he did not show any of these traits on arrival as he opened up to Sarah and myself

immediately. When Rex arrived, he was quick to welcome him, and they both got along instantly and still do.

The same occurred with every new patient that came along. He became inseparable from Davis and the two are best of friends despite their large difference in age. They have a sibling-like dynamic.

He continues to engage with the other patients like family and shows no signs of the claimed social anxiety.

Patient: Rex
Age: 15
Gender: Male
Likes: Loud Music, Solitude, Burgers
Dislikes: Anything Abbey related, also snakes
Reason for Visiting:
State order, family abandoned him and he wasn't adapting to the foster systems.

Notes:
Upon Rex's initial arrival he was calm and collected. He was quiet but friendly. He gets along well with Tristan as well as Sarah and I.

When Abbey first arrived the two had pleasantries together. However, it quickly became known to everyone that the two had vastly different personalities and the two simply cannot seem to understand one another. If Abbey is involved, Rex will be resolved to not participate even to the detriment of himself. We seldom see him for group meals and activities because of this. Most of his meals are left outside his room or, on the rare occasion when he answers, hand delivered by Sarah.

Aside from Abbey, he gets along with everyone else fine and I believe he and Davis have had a few heart to hearts since his arrival. Though usually in the dead of night at the lake or on the roof.

Through various sessions it came out his family abandoned him and he refused to be moved. Despite the state getting involved Rex fought back in order to remain in his family residence. He was later forcefully removed. According to their records he was hostile, aggressive, and threatened staff and others. He was successful in multiple runaway attempts, but always returned to his family residence. He was eventually sentenced by law to come here until he can become a good member of society, or he will end up in a mental hospital.

Patient: Abbey

Age: 20

Gender: Female

Likes: Gardening, Reading, Talking

Dislikes: Rex, ignorance, attitude, the lake

Reason for Visiting:

~~She checked herself in to help combat dealing with abandonment after her recent partner left her behind.~~

She checked herself in for help facing her own past trauma wherein her parents abandoned her at their old lake house.

Notes:

Abbey was the third to arrive. She gets along with Tristan well, though she doesn't go out of her way to interact with him.

She and Rex are complete opposites. While Rex is resolved to stay as far away from her as possible, Abbey on the other hand seems resolved to go out of her way to force interaction between them. She believes everyone can like her if given the chance and thinks Rex has not given them much of an opportunity.

She has little to no interaction with Davis.

She has been known to help Sarah in the kitchen from time to time, though spends most of her time in the library or the garden. It is worth noting that Abbey will refuse to go to the lake as it reminds her too often of her own abandonment. She does yell from a distance at Tristan to be careful.

Her abandonment has had a lasting impact on her. She was abandoned as a child and grew up in a foster system. She was released into the world at 17 as she had given enough proof to the state that she is responsible. Having a stable job, she was able to secure a new residence near work and school. Later she entered a relationship with someone. That person stopped answering their calls and wouldn't answer their door. Abbey was heartbroken as it caused a resurfacing of her child-hood trauma and caused her mental health to spiral. She was put on leave at work and became a shut in. Eventually, she heard of this place and reached out to Sarah and I.After our last big session she said she would take better strides in finding a way to communicate with Rex since some of their relationship with their parents is similar.

Patient: Davis

Age: 27

Gender: Male

Likes: Observation, Theory, Medicine

Dislikes: Not having the answers

Reason for Visiting:

Davis brought himself here in the hopes of finding himself. He mentioned on his application that the humdrum of his job has taken its toll. He says he is at war with himself and feels like he has no sense of identity or aspirations for the future anymore.

Notes:

Davis is calm and collected and so far hasn't shown any signs of temper. In fact, it is most concerning how collected he is at all times. It seems to me that while he is physically present, his mind is often somewhere else entirely. The only time he appears to be completely present is when he is with Tristan.

Through his time with Tristan, he has now become indispensable to the boy. The two are practically inseparable. He spends much of his time listening to and engaging in Tristan's imagination and ideas. In some ways, I would say that Davis is the student and Tristan the teacher. That little boy seems to awaken something in Davis that he thought he had lost long ago.

He also gives Rex counsel, though, in the dead of night at the lake. It seems this is a comfortable place for the two to speak, especially for Rex. I've asked him in the past why he walks the grounds at night, but often don't get more than a shrug. Through my own observation he seems to do much self-reflection. He will just sit out by the lake and stare for hours or lay in the grass and stare at the stars in the night sky. It reminded me of my years studying medicine. When I'd need a break from the stress I'd often go out of the town and find a quiet place to camp for a few nights.

He and Abbey do not interact all that much. Even when in the same space there is very little interaction between the two. In some ways I'd argue that it's as if they don't even exist to one another. They just seem devoid of one another.

Patient: Sarah
Age: ??
Gender: Female
Likes: Cooking, Tea, Talking
Dislikes: bugs, grime
Reason for Visiting: Employee

Notes:
Sarah has been with me since this place first came to be. Together we

take care of the patients. She provides all meals, cleans rooms, cleans the estate, and is often seen as a confidant by many of the patients.

She originally worked at the hospital I interned at. When I finished my time there and completed my studies, I asked her to join me in this venture. She was delighted to work so closely with patients on a more regular and one-to-one basis.

She and Abbey have a mother daughter-like relationship. Abbey will talk Sarah's ear off for as long as she will listen. The two frequently share a private snack time together and have taken trips through the garden or nearby meadow of flowers. She lends an ear and offers advice to others as well.

She adores Tristan and, in many ways, treats him like her own son.

Patient: Bram Finch a.k.a. 'Doctor'
Age: 39
Gender: Male
Likes: Medicine, Helping Others, Literature
Dislikes: Liars
Reason for Visiting: Practitioner of the Valley

Notes:
~~I am Awesome.~~
I studied medicine, herbology, and psychology at Cawmmerce Academy. From being able to understand how the human body and mind work to mixing up a package of pick me ups, I am well versed in my fields of study. This allows me quite a bit of knowledge in assisting a variety of patient needs.

I spend much of my days being available and acting, more often than not, as a headmaster or dorm manager. I believe in allowing a person the freedom to explore themselves freely with little direction. Hence why we encourage our patients the option to join the group for meals. We also leave it up to the patients to accept a session request. They're welcome to schedule their own, but I often try to do impromptu visits. I feel this provides a less stressful and more authentic interaction.

During sessions I simply listen and give subtle nudges in a direction to assist with a patient finding an answer. I believe finding answers oneself leads to a more fulfilling and lasting end result.

I've recently been having strange dreams regarding a castle and a nightmarish figure wielding a massive scythe with bright blood red eyes.

I've recently visited the sky above the valley and have been reintroduced to "my reason for being made". However, why is unclear, but what is clear is that the patients are the answer.

As I read what I've written down, I'm aware that it sounds like I may be slipping but it is the truth of the matter. No matter how hard a pill it is to swallow.

He let out a large yawn and a stretch after reviewing all that he had set before himself. Taking a sip of his coffee, his face scrunched up in disapproval as he discovered it was now cold. He stood  went to get another cup from downstairs. Locking his door as he left his room and continued down to the kitchen, he walked by Rex's room, which was unusually quiet today. He hovered for a moment wondering if he should take the opportunity to check in but did not want to intrude. He had his own work to get back to anyway and chose to continue downstairs. When Rex wanted company, he usually left the door open slightly. As he came to the kitchen, he heard laughter coming from the entry hall. He poured himself another cup from the pot and made his way towards the sounds.

There he found Sarah and all the others standing in front of the manor doors, open, happily speaking with someone. Even Rex and Abbey were in attendance with smiles and positive attitudes. The light that danced in through the windows made the scene feel whimsical.

"My goodness everyone. What has you all so captivated? Do you mind if I join in?" The Doctor spoke over the group, excited to see everyone together. They all turned to him grinning ear to ear and parted to let him through. As they did the Doctor's attention turned to find a new little boy looking back towards him.

"Oh, well, who is this?" the Doctor asked with a smile before taking a sip from his cup.

"Ah, Doctor, this is our newest arrival," Sarah replied as she clapped her hands together in excitement.

She loved when new patients came to the manor. She stepped behind the boy, placing her hands on his shoulders, and walked toward the Doctor. The boy couldn't have been more than ten. He had messy medium length brown hair, eyes as blue as the sky, and a smile that could make the grumpiest of people change their disposition.

The Doctor turned his head to the side in slight confusion.

*I didn't have anything on my calendar for a new arrival.*

"Well, welcome, welcome! It seems everyone has greeted you already. Have you been properly introduced yet?"

"Not yet," the boy replied. His voice was soft and filled the listener with warmth when he spoke.

"All right then, everyone please introduce yourself," the Doctor directed. The others all lined themselves up in order of arrival.

"Hi, I'm Tristan! I love to play outside, and bugs are awesome! I hope you'll come play with me sometime! The lake is one of my favorite places to go!" he rattled off with excitement.

"'Sup, little dude. Name's Rex, but you can call me King Awesome, because well, heh, I'm awesome." Rex said arrogantly while striking a pose. The Doctor gave him a stare. "Or you can call me Rex or whatever . . . I guess . . . " Rex grumbled.

The Doctor let out a playful sigh as he shook his head and looked over to Abbey.

"Hi. My Name is Abbey and I love spending my time in the library or out in the garden. There are so many beautiful flowers that Sarah has planted out there that I hope you'll come to love it too. Oh, and everyone here really loves playing down by the lake, but I think it's kind of freaky, especially at night. But, I guess it's cool if you like it. Oh, and Sarah makes the most wonderful food here, you will love it, I promise! And . . . " Abbey would've kept going had the Doctor not held a hand for her to pause.

"Sorry, I'm big into talking, but I am working on letting others particip-ate in a conversation," she apologized, giving the boy a smile as she wrapped up.

"That's kind of how you have a conversation," Rex blurted out. The group turned to look at Abbey and braced for what was to come. Abbey simply agreed and nodded at him. The room was awkwardly speechless for a moment.

The Doctor broke the silence motioning to Davis with his coffee cup. "And last but not least."

"Oh, um, hello. My name is Davis. I spend most of my time walking around the estate or spending time with Tristan down by the lake," he said plainly.

"Give us a little more, Davis. What's something you like?" the Doctor encouraged as he took another sip.

Davis furrowed his brow in unease and looked at the ground for a moment trying to come up with something.

" . . . I like . . . bread?" he finally said, his voice raising as the question escaped him. He cocked his head to the side. His expression appeared bewildered as he thought about his own answer.

"Me too!" shouted Tristan, throwing his hand in the air above his head, eyes closed, a large toothy smile plastered across his face.

"Yeah, bread is baller, man," Rex said as he crossed his arms, nodding in approval.

"Guys, don't mention food I am starving as it is," Abbey said with sadness as her stomach let out a grumble.

"Well, I think I can take a hint," Sarah shrugged with a chuckle. "I'll go get lunch ready. Apparently, bread will be our main course today." She giggled as she turned to leave. Everyone else broke out into laughter while Davis' cheeks flared red with embarrassment.

"Before we go though, could you tell us your name?" the Doctor said to the new arrival.

"Of course." The boy smiled. "I'm Atticus."

"What should we do?" the first figure dressed in black asked.

"I don't know. What do you wanna do?" the second figure dressed in white returned.

"The kid went to the manor."

"Yes."

"Isn't that bad?"

"Hard to say really," The figure in white said, grasping his chin as he thought.

"Well, if we aren't going to do anything about the kid shouldn't we go look for that other thing?"

"Why bother?" It shrugged.

"Uh, what do you mean why bother? Are you off your rocker, old man?" the figure in black growled.

"No, I want you to tell me why you think that's a smart idea."

"Uh because," It barked at the question.

"That's not an answer."

"Yes it is!"

"People only say that when they're not educated enough to speak."

"Dude, rude."

"There is no point in hunting it. They'll reveal themselves in due time and when they do that'll be our cue."

"Fine, fine . . . " The figure in black finally agreed. He took a seat beside the figure in white, eyes canvassing the forest. "Can we at least like order a pizza or something?"

"Who is going to deliver a pizza to the middle of a forest?"

"Pizza House?"

" . . . . "

"Papa Steve's?"

" . . . . "

"Dotted Squares?"

"I'm not ordering a pizza! You can have the other half of my tuna sandwich in my bag."

"UGH why are you so old!?" The figure in black groaned, elongating the 'o' as it slapped its hands against its face. The grass behind him rustling as he fell onto his back.

# CHAPTER 7

**Diary Entry xx-01-xxxx**

I decided to start writing this diary to track something that's been bothering me. A few months ago, I awoke from a dream. I was covered in sweat and my chest ached. Nothing felt out of place in my room though but . . . inside everything felt twisted and wrong. I do not know how to explain it, but things just felt different . . . as if someone . . . something . . . no . . . that's too wild a claim . . . .

Well, whatever. I got another job lined up for tomorrow. A hefty payday is coming my way. I just need to get this one done, and I'll be set for a bit. This job is getting to get to me in a bad way. I think I need a break.

**Diary Entry xx-02-xxxx**

It has been a few weeks since I first wrote, but it happened again last night. I had another dream that left me with unease. I was short of breath, clenching my chest, my heart racing, feeling, like it was on fire, but I couldn't recall what had caused me to awake so.

Maybe the stress of these recent jobs is getting to me. I never take time off and the last few have been . . . well . . . taxing to say the least. I have no problem doing a job involving adults, but when kids get mixed in . . . well . . . it gets to be a bit much. Far too much if I'm being honest with myself. I really have to disconnect in order to do what I'm hired to do and even then . . . it's the memory that becomes a problem.

Maybe it's stress? Maybe I should start adding limitations to incoming requests.

Wait . . . why should I care? I'm just doing my job. Right? Casualties of war aren't uncommon. What does it matter if they're cut down by me, or left to the elements? People live. People die. At least in this way I get paid.

So why is it bugging me so much?

Why do I feel so much weight lately . . . ?

**Diary Entry xx-03-xxxx**

I had this dream again.

I keep waking up lately having this dream. It's never the same. It's always different. But, the feeling is the same. I can't put a picture or a face or anything to it, but I can tell in my dream that it's the same. It just gives off the same energy, or aura, or whatever you want to call it. I just can't put my finger on it though.

What are my dreams trying to tell me?

Maybe I'll hit the pub tonight. Clearly, I need something to take the edge off. This has been going on for months now. What's wrong with me?

**Diary Entry xx-04-xxxx**

I feel like my mind and my heart are exploding. Last night was the worst night of them all. I felt like I've been completely at war with myself lately and these dreams have not been bringing me any peace of mind. Yesterday I actually questioned whether I should be taking a job. I questioned it because of the targets. What do I care? Why do I care!? It's a job. It's easy money! Take down the convoy and burn the goods. It's not even hard, but I turned it down. I said no. What the hell? It was a direct request for my services. Why would I do that? Why!? The amount of gold I turned down is insane. After all I've done this far, why do I do that?

**Diary Entry xx-05-xxxx**

I don't know how to start this.

I am so confused.

I am so lost.

That convoy job I mentioned in my last entry, the one I turned down. Well, I turned it down because I knew it involved attacking a convoy that had kids. Just a small mom and pop merchant shop trying to get by in the city. But a big timer put a hit out and was willing to pay through the roof for it. They even paid half up front. I turned it down because it "felt like the right thing to do." What garbage. What self-ideology did I choke on that my mind went this direction?

But I feel drawn to the sight anyway.

I heard someone else picked it up. Someone else is going to go after this small family for some quick cash. I don't know why I care but my soul is screaming for me to go there. While my mind shakes its metaphorical head in disapproval at myself. I don't know what I'm doing here, I don't know why I care. I feel so lost and confused these days and rather than continue to fight myself I just decided to follow my heart for once.

So, I am. I'm here. I'm writing this as I wait near the designated location for the convoy to come, and we will see who arrives. I don't know why I'm here . . . but, oh, speak of the devil. Here comes the convoy. Let's see what's about to go down.

**Diary Entry xx-05-01-xxxx**

It just happened.

The convoy came, and out popped the hired help. I watched them stop the convoy. There were five or six guys, some looking tough, and a couple scrawny people with knives and scarves pulled over their nose and mouths to hide behind. They all came out threatening the convoy and the driver, must've been the dad. He had called for his family to stay inside and to not come out. The ringleader, Barthos I think his name was, ordered them to come out or they'd kill their father.

And so, they came.

The wooden door of the cart creaked open as the mother and children fearfully stepped out. Eyes wide in confusion . . . in fear.

They lined them up on the side of the road. They started going through the contents of the convoy. Cut open some bags of grain and rice. Threw pots. Smashed some crates. Breaking and taking whatever the family had inside. When they were done, they set it ablaze. One of the kids reached out crying towards the cart. But were pulled back by their mother. Poor kid . . . .

I wasn't going to bother with this. It was a simple shake down meant to send fear through the family. You see this kind of thing all the time from bigger businesses. They try to elbow out the new competition like this. I was preparing to pack up when one of the scrawny little bastards ripped one of the kids away from their parents. He held the poor thing by their collar and pressed a knife against their throat. The parents pleaded for them to let their child go, tears rolling down their face saying they'd do anything. Barthos didn't even bat an eye and told the thug to do whatever he wanted and went back to chat with someone in a robe who had come out of the tree line. I saw Barthos get paid in full and together they laughed at the destruction his group had caused.

Next that thug's eyes became deranged, opening wide he licked his lips and he tried to walk off with the child away from the scene. He was pulling and dragging the kid by the back of their shirt, while the parents were forced to watch on in horror, screaming, crying, and pleading, all being held captive at knife point.

I don't know how, and I don't know why but that little kid made eye contact with me, reached out their hand out with tears streaming from their eyes, in a muted sound they mouthed "please" and for some reason it rang out in my head. A siren screeching at full volume went off in my mind alerting my senses to sit and be complacent no longer.

Before I could think my body rushed to the scene.

As I flew down the hill and across the road I stepped up behind the thug before he could even realize what was happening. I took his arm and bent it back behind him pointing the dagger into his own back causing him to drop the child. He screamed out in pain as I forced his arm to shove his own dagger into his spine and harshly removed it, tossing it away behind us. Blood splashed onto me and the dirt below him. A moment later his body crashed to earth with it. His eyes filled with confusion, with anger, as he started gasping for air.

He had the audacity to say, "You'll pay for this!" His eyes filled with fire as he glared at me, blood continuing to spill from his wound.

"Pay? I'm here to collect," I said back to him as I stomped on his throat hearing the bones break beneath my foot. A gasp and a wheeze squeezed out of his mouth before his eyes rolled into the back of his head.

The child looked up at me, their tears stopping, petrified, from the shock of what just happened. I looked them in the eyes and told them they'd be okay as I turned my attention to the rest of the group.

The other thugs holding the parents had finally caught up with what was happening, but it was too late. I had already started my assault, stomping wildly in their direction as I hunted my new prey and before their mouths even opened to speak, I was behind them. I did the same move to the one thug holding the mother, only this time I kept the dagger as I removed it. The thug collapsed to the ground letting out a scream and his partner turned just in time to see the dagger I had thrown pierce his face, resting firmly between his eyes. His eyes crossed looking at the blade before his body fell to the ground, releasing the father as he fell.

The parents stared at me as they absorbed how I mercilessly slayed the thugs that were keeping them captive.

"Go." I told them as I gave a nod in the direction of their child. They nodded in acknowledgement and ran off, embracing the kid as they arrived.

After this I laid waste to the rest of the troupe and started walking towards the tree line where Barthos and the robed figure was. Barthos apparently hadn't heard the cries of his crew, but I ended his group in a little less than a minute. And now he too would meet the same end.

The robed figure pointed at me causing Barthos to turn, but as he did, I was already sprinting towards him.

I had collected a few more of their daggers and threw them with as much force as I could muster. For whatever reason this entire ordeal filled me with the rage of someone who was losing their own loved ones and I used that rage as fuel for my fire.

Three daggers found their way into the man's chest all in the split second of turning to see what the robed figure was pointing out. As I arrived at the man, I removed two of them and slammed each one into the side of his neck. I let go, briefly, turning my hands upwards as I regripped the blades handles and pulled them back toward me swiftly, blood rushing out of the freshly carved skin.

"Well look at that, Barthos, I've just given you a lovely set of gills, my bottom feeding friend." I said to him smugly, his eyes wide in shock.

And with that his body fell under its own massive weight as blood steadily gushed from the holes in his neck.

The robed figure let out a yelp and tried to make a run for it, turning towards the woods.

I am one to play with my prey, so I let him run off for a few seconds as I readied my next attack. Throwing the daggers they sang past his ears as the blades conveniently missed their target. His breathing was hard, labored, and loud as he tripped into a tree. He caught himself with his hands but the stumble still sent his shoulder slamming into the thick trunk. He turned to check on me and when he saw I was still in pursuit he gasped. His high-pitched squeak spilling from his lips as he decided to run into the woods

I caught up to him and began to grow bored of watching his pitiful attempts of fleeing. Grabbing his robe by the bottom I caused him to trip and slam face first into the grass below. I pressed the heel of my boot firmly between his shoulders, his spine letting out a crack as I bent down, repositioned my foot, and rested my knee against the back of the man's head.

"Hi." I dragged out the greeting mockingly.

"Get off me!" He grunted, as he tried thrashing himself loose.

"Who ordered the hit?" I growled, knowing the name that was provided to me before wasn't a real one. The man shook his head refusing to answer. So, I gave him some encouragement and I slammed one of those fine daggers in the back of his hand, pinning it into the soil. He was about to scream, so I placed the other one against his cheek guiding the tip just to the corner of his mouth, a warning to start taking me seriously.

"I'm not a big fan of yelling, my man. So, I'd think twice about screaming in agony if you want to live to see tomorrow."

The man's bottom lip went white with how hard he clenched it.

"I'm only going to ask once more. Who requested the hit?" I commanded tilting the tip of the blade into his cheek.

The man whispered the name "Domino".

I was familiar with the name. Rumors of this scumbag are all over the pubs and such.

To make this diary entry shorter the man told me Domino had been impacted regularly by this mom-and-pop shop and was willing to pay 50,000 coins to whomever could end them. I thanked the man and sent him back to Domino with a little message. Though, hopefully he doesn't bleed out before getting back to him. I took his entire left arm as a warning to the man to stop his connection with Domino, and to let Domino know that the Harbinger of Shadows is coming for him.

Heh, I even waved goodbye to the poor fellow with his own hand. Like it or not, I've earned a title for my success and discretion when it came to jobs. *No job was impossible for the Harbinger of Shadows.* I got this name for my efficiency, my silence, and attire. Many people knew my title, far fewer knew my appearance.

After he ran off, I went back to Barthos and collected the 25,000 coins and then I returned to the family. They cowered behind the father, obviously. I was covered in blood and dressed all in black. They also just watched me murder a handful of men. My actions and attire don't exactly scream *friendly person over here.*

"T-t-thank you," the man said, his voice quaking with fear.

"Hold out your hand." I said pointing at him with a bloody dagger. His family started to whine and flinched away at my request.

"You-you-you don't have to do this!" the man's voice pleaded as tears welled up in his eyes. I was growing bored of this day and glared at him as I told him once more. "Hold. Out. Your. Hand."

He turned his head away from me and closed his eyes. In his open hand I dropped the bag of coins. He jolted forward, as he fell into the dirt. He wasn't expecting me to drop anything in his hand, let alone something heavy sack.

"This is the payment that man received to kill you all. You'll find 25,000 coins." I said coldly.

"Kill us?" His eyes grew wide as his mouth hung open.

"Who wants to hurt us? We aren't anyone?" the mother questioned holding her child closer.

"A man named Domino. Seems your business has been taking away 'his' sales. He wanted you out of the picture."

The family whispered back and forth.

"I recommend you leave town and start over."

But the family, all together, chimed in with a loud, "No. We won't."

"Why?" I raised an eyebrow in surprise, confused as to why they'd put themselves at risk again.

"We won't back down from this Domino. With these coins we will rebuild and hire help." They all agreed with the father's statement.

I was oddly moved by their sentiment. I thought I'd be more irritated by such a stupid response, but I wasn't. If anything, I was happy to see their resolve in the face of such adversity.

"Pretty bold move." I said, crossing my arms with a smirk. "Fine. I'm in."

With that I made an agreement to help the family out. I'd be their muscle for trade routes, and they'd keep hired staff at and around their shop back in town.

I don't know why I got involved or made the deal I did. But, it felt right.

*It was the right thing to do.*

None of this mattered until I started having those dreams. Did I do the right thing? I like to think so . . . but why does that matter? My head is so heavy and hot. My mind in a fog. I feel like I'm just fumbling and tumbling not knowing where or what to do. What is wrong with me?

# CHAPTER 8

It had roughly been about a week since the newest arrival, Atticus, had arrived at the manor. In that time the entire energy of the manor shifted. It went from a rather neutral feeling of energy to feeling at ease. Was it the arrival of Atticus or just a coincidence? The Doctor stood at the window in his office looking out towards the lake. He noticed they were all there together, playing and laughing, enjoying one another's company. Rex and Abbey had seemed to bury the hatchet. The Doctor was surprised to see Abbey had pushed past her fears and went to the lake with the others. Right down onto the beach. They were chatting with one another about who knows what. The ripples spread far out across the lake after each of the tones they threw into it.

Taking in the view of the entire valley he could also see Sarah sipping from a cup, most likely tea, as she watched the patients laugh and be merry with each other. Akin to a mother watching her children play. The sun sat high in the sky, the temperature rather comfortable as well. Soft, white, inviting clouds slowly drifted across the vast blue sky.

His thought was interrupted as a knock came at the door.

"Come in!" he called back, his eyebrows raised in surprise as it had appeared everyone was down at the lake.

The door opened, revealing a smiling Atticus.

"Good morning, Doctor. Taking in the sights, are we?" he asked after noticing him by the window.

The Doctor scratched the back of his head giving a smile.

"Ha, you caught me," he admitted with a soft chuckle.

"Wouldn't it be better if we took a walk through them?" Atticus invited.

"You want to take a walk of the grounds?"

*Now that I think about it, even though he has been here a week I do not remember giving him a tour of the place. That is something I've done with every new patient. Wait a minute, did I even hold an introductory interview session within his first few days?* The Doctor squinted his eyes as he tried hard to remember if he had done any of those things, but the answer just seemed unreachable for some reason.

"Yes, that'd be great. After all, we've yet to have any kind of session." He smiled warmly.

And there it was. The Doctor must not have done it.

*How could I let that slip past me?* He scrunched his brow mentally scolding himself.

"I bet that kind of thing doesn't normally get past you." Atticus chuckled.

*Is this kid reading my thoughts or something?* The Doctor's expression softened as he turned his head to look at Atticus. The boy just kept smiling.

"Come on." He motioned towards the Doctor and away they went.

As they headed down the hall they stopped outside of Rex's room.

"Whose room is this?" he asked, but in a way that made it seem like he already knew the answer.

"This is where Rex has been staying," the Doctor replied as his eyes took in the door once more. The words *DIE* still present. His expression went dull as he let out a small sigh.

"The hot headed one who prefers to be alone?" He asked.

" . . . yes."

*How did he know that? Rex hasn't shown any of this behavior during the time of his arrival.* He stared at Atticus from the corner of his eye.

"Say how did you. . . "

"Pretty easy to tell. Him and Abbey do not get along well. Though, you might not be able to tell that with how they've been acting these last few days.," Atticus added.

"Yes, you're right. You're very observant for one so young." He scratched his stubbled chin.

A large smile overtook him as if this was an amusing reply.

"I guess I am," Atticus replied as he started walking away.

They made their way downstairs, pass the kitchen and stopped in front of the library.

"And speaking of Abbey this is her preferred spot, isn't it?" he asked as he walked into the library gazing up and around at the books and curtains.

"Uh, yes. She loves to spend her time reading here. It has a nice view of the garden that she fancies. If she is not in here, she is usually out there." He motioned towards the flowers in the garden outside the window.

He simply smiled back at me. Walking out of the library, we then continued on his walk.

Soon they were in the kitchen.

Atticus took a deep inhale of the aromas seeping out of the place.

"Mmm, now this takes me back." he said, his eyes closed, as he let the aroma linger at his nose a moment longer.

"You too? It smells like Sarah is working on some honey nut bread again. She has a recipe just like my mother used to make." The Doctor smiled, fondly remembering the taste and smell.

"Your mother?" he asked, looking up at the Doctor.

"Yes," he replied gently.

"I see," Atticus said, his eyes stretched wide with playful curiosity.

They continued through the kitchen and outside. There they took the dirt walkway down towards the lake and the beach. The path brought them down a hill only to be brough back up a smaller one. The path wound through the tall grassy scenery. As they arrived at the shoreline there was no one to see. Not a sound in the air, not even of the insects that usually deafen most noises at this time of day. The Doctor looked around to try to see if he could find them, but alas, his gaze never came upon them.

"And what of Tristan and Davis?" Atticus asked.

"What of them?" he asked back, his eyes still searching through the grass and hills.

"What is their relationship, Doctor?"

"They act as if they are siblings most would think. Tristan is an excitable, impressionable child who wants nothing more than to play. It just so happens that Davis has the time for him, and I think the two have created quite a unique bond together. At least, compared to his other options for company. Abbey is often wrapped up in herself, making her too busy to pay attention to the mind of a child. Rex is well . . . Rex and while he will acknowledge Tristan when spoken to, he doesn't go out of his way to engage with him. I suppose Sarah looks after him well, but she's always busy with work and can't spend every minute with him." The Doctor realized he was sharing too much information. Far too much, especially with another patient.

*What am I doing? Why did I just blurt all of that out? When he asked me that question, my body just willfully let the details out. Why?* He clamped his hands together to try and steady his own thoughts.

"And now that I'm here?" he asked.

He continued to have this aura of asking the Doctor questions he seemed to already know the answers to.

*Was this some kind of test for me?* He thought as they continued.

"It is," he replied.

"Excuse me?" the Doctor asked as his eyes widened in surprise, turning to face him.

"You asked if this was all some sort of test for you and I am telling you that it is," he stated not looking at the Doctor as he continued to walk.

Despite the magnitude of what he said the Doctor felt comforted by the child's presence.

"How did you . . . " But before the Doctor could finish, Atticus held up his hand.

"Come with me once more," he said as a blinding light filled the Doctor's vision. Blinking to restore his vision as the light faded, he saw that white, translucent, crystal steps had taken shape before them. The steps did not connect to one another but were spaced apart enough to resemble a staircase, spiraling, upwards into the clouds.

"This way." Atticus instructed as his feet left the ground. They didn't leave the ground to begin walking, no, he had started levitating and then began a casual ascension to the skies above the smile never leaving his face as he rose through the clouds and out of the Doctor's sight.

A lump formed in the Doctor's throat, and he swallowed hard to clear it away. He lifted and placed his foot firmly onto the first step and as he did, a humming sound occurred and suddenly a breeze kicked up and blew past him. He closed his eyes at the unexpected gust and looked back only to see nothing but the sky and a sea of clouds. This was like that dream he had before, and much like that dream, when he looked below his feet he saw the valley below. Only this time he was not looking down at the valley below. This time the valley was fragmented. As if it was just one big chunk of earth floating in a white sea. He turned his attention skyward again only to see cloud after cloud. Taking his next steps, he began the climb skyward. With each step the stair would let out a soft glow and hum as his feet contacted the steps. As he climbed further the steps behind would begin to disappear, removing any pathway back down.

Higher and higher he went. The sky slowly changed as he made his way up the staircase. The journey began with the sky around him at a mid-day blue and then as his journey brought him upwards it became a sunset. Soon dusk and then nightfall. Galaxies and stars filled the vast skyscape around him. Swirls of multicolored constellations could be seen in almost any direction you looked. Shooting stars on occasion tore through the scenery. As the Doctor continued the stars began to go out one by one until they disappeared from sight and then as he neared the top, dawn had come.

The end of the stairs brought him to a floor similar to the stairs, only this was the size of a large room. As he stepped onto the surface Atticus greeted the Doctor with the same familiar smile.

"Welcome back, Doctor," he said arms open.

"Where is this place?" he asked, looking around. According to Atticus, he had been here before but the only part he seemed to remember from the dream was being above the valley. But in that version, it was part of the earth. Not broken into this tiny chunk of floating earth left in a sea of light.

"Why am I here?" The Doctor asked as his gaze returned to Atticus.

His smile lingered as he let out an audible "Hmm."

"Come." Atticus' voice called for him to approach and he stepped forward. Atticus turned, his hand guiding the Doctor to stand beside him. When the Doctor came up beside Atticus five lights brightly appeared. As they faded, five bodies lay sleeping before them.

The first display was of Sarah and Tristan floating lifelessly together, hand in hand.

The second was of Rex, irritation across his sleeping face.

The third was Abbey, her brows arched in sadness.

And last was Davis who laid they're with a neutral expression.

"What is this?" the Doctor asked looking over the sleeping patients.

"Your purpose" Atticus replied softly.

The Doctor tilted his head to the side as he thought for a moment, turning to meet Atticus' eyes.

"My reason for being made?"

"Yes! That's right." Atticus clapped in gleeful acknowledgement.

"I don't understand." The Doctor shook his head.

Atticus held his hand up in the direction of the displays and from their chests different colored lights began to glow.

"These vessels were your purpose Doctor. Harvesting these crystal essences was your charge," he said as the colors lifted from the display bodies and floated towards Atticus above his open hand; yellow, green, red, blue, and purple.

Atticus then closed his hand around the five small crystals. His gaze lifted to the Doctor, giving him another smile. Before he could respond the daylight sky was now dark. From the horizon a bright blood red moon rose, stopping high above them and eclipsing the sun. Red light dampened the space around them.

"THERE YOU ARE ATTICUS, I'VE WONDERED WHERE YOU'VE BEEN HIDING."

A monstrous voice roared through the air around them causing the Doctor to wince. Atticus opened his other hand motioning for him to stay still as they both looked throughout the sky. Atticus finally pointed at a spot above them, and they saw a dark figured man just sitting above them. Looking back at them were those same pulsing red eyes the Doctor had been seeing in his nightmares. A gasp escaped his throat and Atticus slipped his hand into the Doctor's and then looked him in the eyes.

"It's going to be okay." Atticus reassured.

"IT'S REALLY NOT."

The voice mocked as it now rose to its feet and reached both its hands over its head, throwing a swirling blade towards the pair. Just like before a door of light opened, this time below them and as they fell through it they stepped near the ranch doors to the manor's kitchen. The swirling scythe was on a crash course for them. If it were not for Atticus' cool and level head steering their course, this might have gone differently. However, he promptly shut the door of light before the scythe could complete its trip.

The sound of breaking glass consumed the world around them and looking skyward they saw the shards of the broken crystal staircase as it fell into the valley, the screeching of the twirling scythe tearing through the sky. It punctured the sandy shore of the lake as it crashed, spraying sand into the air and out into the grassy fields.

As the sand settled the pair did not stick around to see what was next and Atticus took the Doctor by the hand turning to run back into the manor.

They searched for a place to hide before the nightmare could catch up. It was not long after the sand fell that another loud crash was heard outside the place. The Doctor scrambled up the stairs, trying to keep up with Atticus as he kept pulling him by the arm to wherever it was that Atticus led them. They finally arrived at one of the bedrooms.

*I should know which room we are in, but . . . I have no clue.* They entered the room and Atticus shut the door behind them.

The Doctor did his best to stay quiet, but his entire body shook with every beat of his heart and fear coursed through him as the walls of the closet suffocated him. His breath felt like a siren going off with each exhale and inhale. He covered his mouth and pinched his eyes shut, hoping it wouldn't find them. Its footsteps grew closer and closer. A deafening clicking came from outside the closet as the door handle began to turn and the door let out a long creak as it slowly opened. The creaking paused for what felt like an eternity before it smashed into the wall. Various pieces of wood pummeling the floor echoed from outside the closet.

*It is here!*

The Doctor's mind screamed, and his eyes shot open. Sweat fell from his face as he tried to remain calm and suppress every sound, every thought, hoping it would keep them safe. He looked to the boy sitting beside him. The boy didn't show an ounce of fear on his face, and he gently rested his hand on the Doctor's knee. His face was serious, and he gave the Doctor a nod acknowledging his fear. The warmth of his eyes eased the Doctor's mind helping to slow its intrusive thought. Their attention pulled back to the door in front of them as the sounds of wood creaking outside of their hiding space polluted their ears. The floorboards let out a groan as it continued searching through the room.

The figure let out an irritated sigh when another crash came from outside the closet.

"COME OUT, COME OUT, WHEREVER YOU ARE!" It growled.

Despite the Doctor's racing heart, he and the boy remained silent.

"I KNOW YOU'RE IN HERE ATTICUS." Its low scratchy voice boomed as a loud screech followed.

"THIS TIME," its voice was abrasive "I'LL BE RID OF YOU FOR GOOD!" It finished in a roar, and they heard more wood splitting from outside the closet.

"HE CAN'T PROTECT YOU! THERE IS NOWHERE FOR YOU TO GO!" Its voice tore through the air beside the closet. Again, the sound of the figure's footsteps polluted the air. Thud after thud; creak after creak. With each step the Doctor's heart pounded harder, his body burning with the heat of fear and adrenaline. Through the cracks of the door, with what little light there was, they saw it. The nightmare. It had stopped its rampant destruction right in front of their hiding spot.

*It's found us.* The Doctor swallowed, emitting an audible gulp.

The thought had just echoed through the Doctor's mind when he heard a terroristic, joyful, chuckle from outside. His gaze pulled upward only to find a pulsing red eye sneering back at him through the cracks.

"FOUND YA."

# CHAPTER 9

**Diary Entry xx-06-xxxx**

It's been a few weeks since I agreed to this partnership and things have been going well. But, today something in me started to stir, and stir for the worse. I guess I should elaborate.

Since my last entries, my mind has felt at ease. Like the decisions I've made were the right ones and they've started me down a new path. Today, things felt different. I started to feel unsure of my decisions again and not just unsure on whether this was good or bad, more so I wanted to do away with these problems. Do away with these people. Just finish the job that Barthos had started.

I don't know why. If that's really how I feel, then why did I get involved in the first place? Why did I stick my neck out? Was it just to mess with Domino? Was it for power? My ego? Greed? I feel so conflicted on my decisions right now and I worry about things that I haven't worried about in years. What is wrong with me? What is going on with me right now? Why does my heart feel so on edge with everything lately? I've never felt so unsure of who I am. It feels like I'm at war with myself and I just can't seem to land on a side.

**Diary Entry xx-07-xxxx**

Today I snapped.

We were making a trip in between towns again, the father and I, and we were ambushed. During the fight I felt the fury inside me snap. Carnal rage came over me and it felt so good.

All I needed to do was just disarm these thugs and then send them on their way, but I did more than that. I did what I did on the day I met this family. I ripped these criminals' apart limb from limb.

I killed them.Mercilessly.

Despite their pleas and their begging, I didn't stop. I killed each and every one of them. It felt good. *Really good.* But, afterwards, after the adrenaline wore off and I was left in the wake of my wrath, the old man said my name and I turned towards him with hate pulsing through my veins. When my gaze met him, I pointed my scythe at this throat, the tip of the blade an inch from his neck. He stood there frozen. He apologized and offered me a rag to clean the blood away from my face. I jerked it from his hand and motioned for us to continue.

I almost killed him, and it felt okay to do so. But then, afterwards, guilt washed over me again, and I knew I had made a terrible mistake.

What did I do?

Why did I do it?

I didn't need to, I didn't want to, or . . . did I? My head hurts. Sweat beading off my forehead as if my body was twisting and turning on the inside. I'm so confused and so lost. My stomach feels like it's just being punted and flipped over and over again. A pain jolted through it like someone just sucker punched me.

I want to vomit.

Who have I become?

What have I become?

**Diary Entry xx-08-xxxx**

I read my last entry and it's almost funny. Why do I care so much? This world . . . these "people" hide away behind their walls, afraid of the monsters and beasts outside, afraid a big baddie might come and get them. Calling on their soldiers and patrols to protect them from the monsters outside. Yet they don't even realize that they're the monsters of this world. Inside their own walls lie the true fiends of this star. They take, and they lie, and cheat, and kill, and only care for themselves. They can't even take care of each other. At least out here, in this *monster infested* world. They have the decency to look out for one another. I'd be doing the creatures of this world a favor if I just axed the rest of humanity. None of them deserve to be here.

None.

Not one.

**Diary Entry xx-09-xxxx**

Did I write that?

Why would I write that?

Do I really think there is no good in this world? The family I work for, even after what they saw me do . . . they still showed me kindness and welcomed me in their homes. We break bread together every night. These are good people. There are good people out there. People like this deserve to live. Deserve a chance to find happiness, to bring happiness to others. They can do it.

But why do I feel so conflicted inside?

Why can I love people one minute and then in the next feel on the verge of losing myself to an uncaged rage and lashing out?

I'm starting to lose control and I think, for the better of others I should leave before I hurt someone I care about. Because I do care. I care about these people. Do you hear that inner me or whatever is inside me? I DO CARE! I WON'T LET YOU HURT THEM!

It's scythe slammed into the closet door and in the next instant, it tore the door from its hinges sending the scrap of wood crashing into the floor behind it, obliterating its rickety form into nothing more than broken shards.

"GOOD TO SEE YOU ATTICUS." The red-eyed nightmare smirked.

"Hello." Atticus replied, raising his hand in front of him in a wave.

Its red eyes pulsed in irritation. A scowl replacing that wicked smile.

Atticus simply smiled back at the creature. He then turned towards the Doctor.

"Come, Doctor. Our ride is here." He extended a hand towards him helping lift the Doctor back to his feet.

"WHERE DO YOU THINK YOU'RE GOING?" It roared, shifting the scythe towards them.

"We don't have time to deal with nightmares right now," Atticus said, waving his hand dismissively. His eyes narrowed, glaring at the nightmare. His expression was one of disappointment. Atticus raised his hand over his head and then snapped his fingers. The noise was louder than one would expect from a mere snap. It caused the Doctor to recoil in surprise and just then another door of light appeared behind them.

The nightmare swung his scythe at Atticus, but it simply passed through him. This took the nightmare by surprise and instead in anger turned its scythe on the Doctor. Before it could complete its swing at the Doctor, Atticus called to him again.

"Just what do you think you're doing?"

"I've been watching this 'doctor' and I know he is the link between the crystal essences. I'm here to sever that link and take back the personas, they belong to me!" He roared.

Atticus gave him a smile and opened his palm.

"You mean these? I've already completed severing the connection," he chuckled as the five crystal shards rested nuzzled together dimly in his hand.

The nightmare swung his scythe towards Atticus again only this time it was successful in landing a blow, swinging the scythe like a bat. Atticus dropped the five shards and the blow sent them flying about the room. Small chimes clamored out as the crystals hit the walls and floors, rolling their way around the room scattering from the nightmare's sight. A smile crept across its face as it laughed at Atticus' mistake. It launched itself back into the room and started throwing furniture in desperation to collect crystals.

"Come along, Doctor," the child said again as he grabbed his hand, leading him into the door of light.

"But Atticus, what about the crystal shards? Don't we need those?" The Doctor called to him looking back to see as the nightmare continued its search for the shards.

*Wait why did I say that? As far as I know, I have no affiliation with those shards. At least not one I can remember. Right now, everything just feels hazy. Almost like an out of body experience. Who am I?*

The Doctor was tugged along as Atticus pulled them through the door. As they stepped through the frame he replied to the Doctor's question.

"No, we have no need for empty vessels."

With a thud, the door closed behind them.

**Diary Entry xx-10-xxxx**

I left a note for the shopkeeper letting him know that it was time for me to go. I had taught them how to fight, how to watch their surroundings, and they no longer needed me. But, as I was about to depart, the old man caught me with my things packed and my traveling clothes set in place.

"So, you're leaving us?" he asked, standing in the doorway of my hut.

I gave a nod. He could see the sadness in my eyes and simply gave me a soft smile.

"I can't say I understand, but we'll miss having you. You helped us more than you can ever know and for that we are eternally grateful." He extended his hand towards me, and I accepted it in a firm shake.

I didn't want to leave . . . but my moods have been so unpredictable of late that I can't stay here in good conscience knowing I'd be putting them at risk. I've had a hard time even keeping my thoughts straight let alone my actions. I can't stay here knowing I could someday snap and do that to them.

I gave him a warm smile, or, as warm a smile as I could make. I felt really torn about this. I know it is better that I go.

I know that.

I've been searching my entire life for a place just like this. A place to call home. A place that has people I can trust and so it leaves my heart heavy as I have to say goodbye, and it hurts more knowing the reason I have to leave is because of me. Because I can't trust myself.

I can't trust myself around anyone anymore.

"Thanks for everything. I know I didn't speak much, but this felt . . . like home," I said with audible sadness.

His eyes widened at my comment and a smile glided from ear to ear.

"I'm glad to hear that, and don't worry I'll tell the others in the morning. You will be sorely missed, Atticus," he said to me.

"As will you all."

We shared a short hug, one hand left in a handshake, and the other swung around the shoulder in a firm grasp and then I took my leave.

This was for the best, and I wish them all nothing but happiness.

As I started down the dirt path with nightfall overhead, I heard him call to me once more.

"Oi, Atticus!" he shouted and so I turned back to see the dim light of my small hut lighting up the entryway. "You'll always be welcome, you hear?"

I lifted my hand to give acknowledgement.

I turned away from him and off I continued into the night.

Alone once more.

It's for the better, I keep reminding myself.

They're safer without me.

They came through the door and the two had stepped into a small wooden shack, the door of light closing once they had. A trio of candles flickered on a table that sat in the center of the room. The Doctor didn't notice right away but at the table sat two figures. One wore a suit, all white in color; his tie, his button up undershirt, all white. Most of his white hair tied back in a low ponytail, but long chunks hung from each side and framed his face, draping down past his chin. This man looked to be middle aged.

The other wore all black and his attire wasn't that much different from the nightmare's. He had messy black hair that covered his eyes and jetted out in all directions. While the one in white had a soft expression, this person wore a harsh, almost taunting expression, and was quite a bit younger. He didn't look much older than a teenager.

"Took you long enough you dumb kid!" the one in black scolded giving the table a firm pound of his fist.

"Lude, stop," the one in white replied. "It couldn't be helped. The nightmare had already discovered him. It was only a matter of time."

"It's true. He needed to be removed if our plans were to be successful." Atticus shrugged at the pair.

"Oh yeah, really successful, weren't you?" Lude mocked as he stood up in a rush. The clonk of his wooden chair echoed into the space as it fell. "Hurray you, you brought us 'the doctor' but forgot the part that actually mattered. You forgot the damn crystals. And not only did you just leave them behind, but you basically gave them to that bastard on a silver platter!" he shouted as bent over into Atticus' face.

"Lude!" the one in white called back.

"What, Farrin? Am I wrong?" he shouted back to the one in white glaring over his shoulder at him.

"You are," Atticus protested as he turned, leading the pair's eyes to the Doctor.

"What? I don't see anything different?" Lude replied impatiently, looking the Doctor up and down while his hands rested on his hips.

Just then the Doctor's chest lit up with light and five different colors emerged from him.

"His job is complete," Atticus replied as the colors of light shined warmly in front of him. The room, and their faces, light up with five different colored pulses.

"My goddess, you did it," Farrin replied.

Lude slapped his hands together, the leather making a deafened clap.

"Well, damn. I take it back. Nice work, kid," he rejoiced smacking Atticus on the back.

Atticus simply smiled at the Doctor as if satisfied with the outcome of recent events.

"Right then, we need to get moving," Lude said as he walked past them.

"Wait a second!" the Doctor called out.

The three turned and looked at the Doctor, Lude glaring with malcontent on being stopped.

"What?" he asked, shrugging at Farrin and Atticus.

The Doctor scoffed and shrugged his shoulders. He looked at Lude, and motioned to Farrin and Atticus.

"Can someone fill me in, maybe? What is that thing?" he pointed outside in the direction of the manor. "What is going on and who the hell are you people?" his voice growing louder with frustration while motioning towards them.

Lude just looked at the Doctor with confusion.

"What is he on about?" He asked, looking past the Doctor to where Atticus stood. "Did you not fill him in on what's going on?" Lude glared as he asked, disbelief in his voice.

"Ah, no," Atticus replied as he looked at the ground.

"Uh, why not?" Lude pressed.

"Well before this all began, I cleared Counticus' memories and affixed upon him a new identity as a doctor." He chuckled a little.

"A what?" Lude grew more irritated as his eyes narrowed at Atticus.

"A doctor," Atticus repeated.

Lude looked over at Farrin in surprise. Who replied with a shrug.

"Why not?" Farrin said as he shook his head.

"Afterall we are the ones who created the *child that never was*. It makes sense when we three failed last time that he would follow a similar path," Farrin said thoughtfully.

"But the *adult that never was*?" Lude questioned in both surprise and frustration as his hand jetted out motioning at the Doctor.

The three of them spoke to one another, but to the Doctor, this was all over his head.

*The Child that never was?*

*The Adult that never was?*

*What are they even saying, what does this all mean?* His head was fuzzy from all this information, and throbbed in pain, feeling as if a hammer was struck against it.

"Ah, his memories are starting to return," Farrin pointed towards the Doctor.

"Well good. Maybe we should explain it to him and speed this along already?" Lude folded his arms.

The three gave a nod at the notion.

"Well, take a seat Doctor . . . I mean . . . Counticus." Atticus motioned for the Doctor to take a seat at the table.

# CHAPTER 10

At the table sat the Doctor, Atticus, and Farrin. Lude stood with his arms crossed in front of him. The was silent as the everyone waited for one of them to begin.

"So . . . "

"You keep . . . " Atticus started talking but the Doctor began at the same time thus interrupting one another.

"Sorry!" Atticus replied.

"My apologies. Please go ahead." The Doctor nodded at Atticus.

"No, you can go. I'm sure you have a lot of questions to ask." Atticus laced his fingers in his lap.

The doctor nodded at Atticus, his eyes examining Farrin, who met his gaze with a warm smile. Meanwhile Lude gave him a side-eye glare and snort.

"Okay," the Doctor said as he cupped his hands together.

*Why am I so nervous?*

"That's natural." Atticus replied.

Atticus had done this several times recently and the Doctor had taken notice.

"How do you do that?" the Doctor questioned.

"Well . . . " Atticus gave a smile while his eyes looked to the ceiling, as if he knew he would get in trouble for replying.

"What's he doing?" asked Lude.

"I can think a thought and then he . . . just knows it. He will answer my internal question without me even saying a word"

"Oh, he can, can he?" Lude grunted as he squinted daggers at Atticus, who just smiled and looked up at the ceiling.

"I can," he admitted after a moment, bringing his gaze back to the Doctor.

"You know no bounds do you, kid? Can't even leave him his own thoughts?" Lude said, irritated as he started pacing around the room.

"Is this normal?" the Doctor asked.

"No, Counticus, it isn't." Lude's voice growled.

"Yes, Lude is correct. Even persona have our set of rules. Typically we are left to our own devices . . . well, usually." Farrin's eyes were closed as he pressed his chin into his knuckles.

"Persona?" The Doctor raised an eyebrow at the word.

"Autonomous personalities," Farrin replied.

"Personalities?" The Doctor gave a puzzled look at the use of the word.

"Yeah, *personalities*," Lude repeated gruffly.

"I don't understand."

"Sheesh, what does this guy know?" Lude glared at Atticus for answers.

"Well . . . I may . . . have completely wiped the memories of all the persona before putting them into the valley and then simultaneously gave them memories from the true Atticus and kind of made them believe they're each individual people and that those memories solely belong to them. While also making them believe they were living life normally in a real world," Atticus stated.

Lude was silent.

"And Counticus?" Farrin raised his eyebrows.

"I basically did the same thing. The desire to be a doctor came from the true Atticus' childhood dreams and I just filled in the rest. Then I removed the memory of his creation and placed him in the valley with the rest." Atticus nodded his head as he finished.

"And I assume the purpose was for the crystals?" Farrin questioned.

"Yes." Atticus snapped his fingers and the colored lights gently glided from the Doctor's chest onto the table before them. There they floated above, pulsing gently from bright back to dim. The colors illuminating the room around them.

"I'm sorry, what?" the Doctor replied.

"And why do you keep calling me Counticus? My name is . . . "

*Why can't I think of my own name?* He clenched his eyes shut as he tried to think back as far as he could. Nothing came before the valley. Even trying to remember his schooling and youth all he could remember was the idea. Not any visible place where he shared the idea. Nothing about friends. Nothing about school life. Growing up. Nothing.

"Why, can't I remember?" His eyes opened partially staring at the table before. His voice slated with sadness.

Farrin let out a sigh while Lude shook his head in disapproval.

"This is why you don't mess with persona, Atticus," Lude scolded.

"Yes. I understand why you chose to make another artificial persona, but you broke some of our strictest of rules and those rules exist to-" Farrin was cut off by Atticus, raising a hand to stop him in the middle of his lecture.

"I know, to ensure the stability of a personality without causing potential harm to the true Atticus. But I didn't have time for that. None of us did. We know what the nightmare can do. We've seen what it's done already," ,e said, snapping his fingers again. Pages manifested in the air and floated around the room. The words on them were read aloud for all to hear as they each lit up.

Why do I care so much? This world . . . these "people" hide away behind their walls, afraid of the monsters and beast tribes outside, afraid a big baddie might come and get them. Calling on their soldiers and patrols to protect them from the monsters outside. Yet they don't even realize that they're the monsters of this world. Inside their own walls lie the true fiends of this star. They take, and they lie, and cheat, and kill, and only care for themselves. They can't even take care of each other. At least out here, in this *monster infested* world. They have the decency to look out for one another. I'd be doing the creatures of this world a favor if I just axed the rest of humanity. None of them deserve to be here.

None.

*Did I write that? Why would I write that?*

*I care about these people. Do you hear that inner me or whatever is inside me? I DO CARE!*

Even Lude's irritated disposition grew sad listening to these words, his eyes dropping to the floor.

"What are these?" the Doctor asked.

"Diary entries." Farrin's words were soft and a bit hollow.

"By whom?" he looked back at Farrin.

Lude and Farrin looked away, sadness taking over their expressions.

"The true Atticus," Atticus spoke softly.

"You keep saying that, but what does that mean?" The Doctor was doing his best to follow this conversation, but all this information went over his head.

"This would've been a hundred times easier if you'd just left Counticus with his memories, you know?" Lude sighed.

"Yes, and if I had done that the nightmare would've found them that much sooner and the essence extraction would've been a failure." Atticus' cheerful tone turned dark and severe.

"If you say so." Lude's expressions softened, raising his hands defensively as he moved away from the kid.

"He's still confused," Atticus said to the room.

"Maybe I should explain the reality of the situation?" Farrin offered.

"Please do," Atticus replied, motioning for him to take the floor.

"Very well," he stretched his neck back and forth. "Brace yourselves though, it's a long explanation."

"All creatures of this world, whether it be human kin, beast kin, monster kin, etc., are all born from the aethers of this world, in the design of the goddess. Once consciousness begins to awaken in the living being two autonomous personalities, or persona, are created at once. The light persona, represented by myself, and the dark persona represent by . . ."

"Me!" Lude poised a thumb against his chest smirking at the Doctor.

Farrin sighed.

"Both are created to keep the interests of the being at the forefront of their life. Light typically tries to keep them on a path of kindness, good unto others, etc. doing things that both the being and others might define as a 'good person' or committing 'good deeds'. While the dark persona keeps focus on the needs and wants of the being."

"To bad everyone sees us as the 'bad guys' though," Lude interrupted.

"Some deem this as a 'selfish persona'," Farrin put emphasis on some as he turned towards Lude. "but truly, a being cannot live in harmony without both persona present. Too much light and you end up self-sacrificing yourself for the 'good' of others which is a detriment to yourself. Too much dark and you become ignorant to the world around you, selfish, and in some cases malicious, greedy, and cruel. The light and dark personas were created to keep one another in balance," Farrin held his hands out as a scale to add a visual aid to this long lecture.

"Which often leads a being to inner conflict as they war with themselves about the age-old questions 'what is right', 'what is wrong'. This happens to all beings big or small. Young or old. As life continues on, additional persona can develop. There are all kinds of persona, and they can be created for many different reasons. To keep it simple, let's review what persona sleep within the being Atticus, or whom we continue to refer to as the true Atticus." Farrin waved his hand across the table. A mini version of each persona from the manor appeared in black and white hues.

"Sleeping inside of Atticus are seven organic persona. His dark and light persona, which is Lude and myself. His five additional persona that were created from childhood to today: Tristan, Rex, Abbey, Davis, and Sarah."

The mini Tristan lit up with color and moved slightly forward ahead of the other mini figures.

"Tristan is depicted by the green essence, which symbolizes his childhood. Green was Atticus' favorite color as a child and this persona was created to embody his imagination, child wonder, play, and curiosity to the world."

Mini Tristan's color faded and it slide back in line. Rex lit up and slid forward.

"Rex is depicted by the red essence which symbolizes his teen years. Atticus had a hard life growing up, and still does to this day. During the time his parents were gone, his home was destroyed, he was just coming into his abilities. It's hard for a kid to take care of themselves and being a survivor of war is difficult. Rex came to be the embodiment of rage and strength."

Lude cleared his throat loudly drawing everyone's attention.

"What?"

"You okay?" Atticus asked.

"I'm fine. Just get on with it!" He flicked his hands toward the table.

"Abbey is depicted by the blue essence which symbolizes peace, self-doubt, and oddly enough, acceptance. In Atticus' young adult years, he uncovered truths about his youth that may have been better left unsolved. Secrets about himself that he never knew . . . or rather came to forget. At this point though he came to realize he didn't 'lose' his parents. They finally succeeded in abandoning him: an effort that took years to accomplish. When he realized this, all the memories he had locked away about being with his parents at the lake, long walks, and such became obvious. They weren't fun trips for their family; they were opportunities and attempts for his parents to rid themselves of 'the monster' they had been cursed with. After this realization Abbey was born and became the embodiment of self-doubt, self-hatred, fear of rejection, and again, oddly enough, acceptance of himself as he one day accepted it for what it was."

"This was a good one." Lude added, Farrin nodded in agreement.

"Why?" the Doctor asked.

"Because this is when we started learning to use sick weapons, dude." He closed his eyes with a smirk while the Doctor looked unsure of what he meant. As expected, an irritated groan came from Lude.

"Sorry Lude," Atticus giggled. "You might not realize it Counticus, but the True Atticus is a mercenary for hire. Not only that, but he's a weapon master!"

"What does that mean?" the Doctor began and Lude slammed his hand into the table.

"It means he is a master of all weapons. Swords and shields, lancers, claws, a-"

"Axes, bows, truly it'd probably be easier to list the weapons he doesn't know how to use," Farrin interrupted. Lude in turn shot him a glare. "Let's get back to it." Farrin chuckled as their attention returned to the figures on the table.

Abbey slid back into place and Davis slid forward.

"Davis is depicted by the yellow essence symbolizing his wayward years. As he began transitioning into adulthood he still struggled with the memories of his past. While he accepted how his parent's saw him, and accepted his powers for what they were, he never was completely at peace with this. In honesty, this persona is the hardest for Lude and I to handle because it goes against both of us. Davis is the embodiment of his 'monster' personality because he truly believes he was a blight on his parent's life and that if he was just normal, he would've had a happy life. You'd think falling into acceptance from Abbey would've set him on a different path of self-love, but it didn't . . . instead it led him here. To a path of hatred and self-blame. A path filled with regret and what if's that would haunt him and start to corrode him from within."

"Parents don't think of the impact of their actions and words can have on their kids. But, those kids are left to carry all that trauma and burden. It's so heavy. Some never recover. And Atticus, hasn't recover from their actions." Lude's voice grew hoarse as he spoke.

Farrin placed a hand on his shoulder, but Lude shrugged it off immediately and turned away from the table.

"Lastly, Sarah is depicted by the purple essence which symbolizes the ideology and imagery Atticus had of his mother. This is a unique persona that was created around the time of Rex and has been present for ages. She alters her behavior based on what Atticus needs. In a way the Sarah persona was created to balance out Rex and as time went on, she came into being the counterweight for Davis. Even though his mother abandoned him, he still remembers the sadness in her eyes and hesitation she had on all those trips. Despite her trying to get rid of him, he acknowledged her own guilt. Honestly, it's a miracle Sarah didn't 'evolve' into what Davis is, but instead Davis was made a separate persona. She is the embodiment of a mother's love. Or at least, what Atticus thinks it should be."

"Wow," the Doctor said.

"Yeah, man. This kid has been through hell." Lude turned back to the group, stuffing his hands into his pockets.

"Yeah . . ."

Farrin cleared his throat softly.

"Now onto our two artificial personas. An artificial persona is when an organic persona makes a persona. As mentioned previously, the living being has persona that are brought into existence based on needs, traumatic events, counterbalances, events that impact the heart, and etc. Persona can be born in someone for any number of reasons. But an artificial persona is a persona who is made by another persona. Atticus, for example, was created by me and Lude. We gave him the name Atticus because we designed him completely off what the true Atticus' appearance was in his childhood. We gave him the same personality as well. We also code-named him 'The Atticus that never was' because if events had gone as they were originally perceived, this is the version of Atticus that would've existed. Sadly, because of the war consuming his home and his parents rejecting him, this Atticus was lost to those events and a new version of Atticus was created. That is what has led to the true Atticus of today."

"Too bad. The world never got the chance to experience this face." Atticus produced a large toothy smile while pointing at his face with both hands.

The Doctor and Farrin both let out a chuckle while Lude rolled his eyes.

"Continue." Lude ordered.

Farrin snorted and looked back at the Doctor.

"We made him to help us with this nightmare situation. At some point in adulthood the true Atticus found himself arrogant, cocky, and behaving more in line with the persona of Davis and Lude. Though I did my best to keep the balance, nothing was working. One day the true Atticus came across word of his parents' whereabouts, so he went to investigate. Atticus came to find his father standing over his mother's corpse. While his father was never one to shy about the topic of getting rid of 'that monster' he always left the task to Atticus' mother. Every time she faltered.

"From that moment on his heart fell into turmoil. Blaming himself for not getting here sooner, for being born, for not being what his parents wanted, for not being able to save the woman who, time after time, saved him from abandonment. It was this juncture in time when a deep darkness, a seed of evil, reached out to Atticus offering him succor and justice for what had happened and so he took his scythe in hand and took his revenge."

"Goodness. I suppose that made you happy then?" the Doctor said as he turned his attention towards Lude.

He didn't realize who the Doctor was talking to in the instant but then it clicked. "Are you talking to me?" He pointed towards his chest.

"Yes."

"What the hell? Why would I be happy?" His eyes narrow from the comment as he balled his hands into fists.

"Well, you're the dark persona. Isn't bad guy stuff kind of your thing?"

"Oh my goddess," Lude stood frozen for a moment. "I'm going to punch you right in your stupid face." He started towards the Doctor, fist cocked ready to strike.

"Lude!" Farrin barked rising to stop his counterpart.

"No, this guy deserves it!"

The Doctor threw his hands up. "Sorry, I just remembered Farrin said dark persona are not 'bad' they just get associated with bad stuff. Sorry!"

"See?" Farrin motioned to the apologetic Doctor.

"Tck, whatever man," his body fell into the chair next to Farrin. "Get your facts straight."

Everyone else sighed in relief.

"Anyway, that evil flourished from the pain of losing his mother. We persona did our best to stop it, but we were overwhelmed. That evil that spoke to him that day led him astray. He was a child of the goddess, born with exceptional abilities, the power of foresight, and from trial after trial Atticus' heart became deaf to our aid or reasoning. Over time only the darkness remained, and his soul was the perfect breeding ground for the nightmare to be placed. We did our best to hold him back. To keep him from taking Atticus, but in the end we failed . . . . When it presented itself, it tried to destroy all of us, the true Atticus' personas. Its goal was to destroy us in order to get to the heart of Atticus. We've been fighting off the nightmare for years now and it's been a struggle."

The three shared a look of exhaustion between each other.

"We've lost the crystals many times. With little hope left Lude and I created Atticus, the child that never was, and to combat the nightmare we ensured he had the memories of what had transpired before his creation. The three of us took the fight to the nightmare to recover the essences of the true Atticus before he could find the core, Atticus' heart. While we succeeded in finding the crystals, we failed in destroying the nightmare. Lude and I were at a loss as to what to do. However, Atticus said he had a plan, so we left him to his schemes."

Atticus gave a nod. "And that's when I made you, Counticus."

"We restored the personas to their forms, their crystals sleeping away inside. Atticus removed their memories and fabricated new ones to create the illusion that all this was in order to protect the personas and you. By removing the memories of who they, and you, were, the nightmare would have a difficult time tracking them down."

"Traversing the human soul and mind is difficult enough, but with the personas not knowing who they are and being hidden away, Atticus bought enough time for you to fulfill your function, Counticus. Atticus created you as a counter step to himself whose purpose is to rid the soul of the nightmare. Your purpose was to become the house for all the persona. Then Lude, Atticus, and I would be able to destroy the nightmare once and for all with our combined powers and keep the true Atticus safe. This would allow the persona to be returned afterwards and provide the true Atticus the steps needed to start healing from his traumatic past and present."

Farrin let out an exasperated sigh and drew a new breath. "That is the gist of everything."

The Doctor sat there staring at the group in a daze, his eyes had glossed over at the lengthy and informative explanation.

*None of this is 'real'? We exist as autonomous personalities, or persona, inside the soul and mind of the true Atticus, a living breathing person? We are created out of necessity for preservation of life due to events and make up the soul of Atticus?*

Atticus nodded.

"That's right. The persona are a collective of autonomous person-alities given shape and mind to assist in a living being's preservation throughout life. We can change, alter, fade, and be born again. Though you and I are exceptions since we are artificial persona made by Lude and Farrin, and you were made by me. Technically they could get rid of us whenever they see fit." He shrugged as he finished the thought.

"Couldn't the true Atticus just alter us on his own?" the Doctor asked.

"Ahh a good question but no, not really." Farrin replied.

"Why not?"

"Lude and I made Atticus together specifically because he would have both the light and dark persona essence influenced upon him. Hence why Atticus does whatever he wants regardless of what the rules are. An unfortunate side effect from processing *both* our essences." He narrowed his eyes as he looked at the child, who closed his eyes and gave him a smile only a child could and Farrin sighed at the scene.

"His sole function is the elimination of the nightmare for the sake of the true Atticus' preservation. In hindsight though, we probably should've given him a different name."

"No kidding," Lude blurted out in a chuckle. "Imagine if this was some kind of story and the audience is like Atticus this, the true Atticus that, the hungry Atticus, the sleep deprived Atticus, ham sandwich eating Atticus, like what else could we name Atticus?" Lude said sarcastically.

Farrin chuckled.

"You can't make this stuff up."

While the two shared a laugh, the Doctor remained in his daze, just staring at the pair, paralyzed by the sudden awareness of the truth of all these events.

"Well, what about those?" The doctor pointed to the floating diary entries.

"Ahh yes, these," Farrin said as he rubbed his chin, thinking for a moment.

"What you're seeing here is the current state of affairs." He motioned to the recent entries that had been read aloud earlier.

"You may have noticed that these entries are wildly contradicting one another to the point where the true Atticus is noticing alterations in his own thoughts and personality."

"That can't be good, right?" The Doctor's eyes widened as he recalled the words written.

"Certainly not," Farrin agreed.

"Definitely not," Lude scoffed, staring at the pages.

"He is at war with himself to a degree vastly beyond what the light and dark persona are meant to bring. His heart, his very soul is in a state of fatigue being strained far beyond the normal level."

"There's a normal balance?" The Doctor raised his brow in surprise, curious to the idea.

"Of course, there is," Lude grunted as he shrugged.

"Yes, as mentioned at the beginning of all of this the light and dark persona are created to establish a balance in terms of self-preservation and doing what's right in the world. Society has labeled these two things as 'doing good' and 'selfishness' and while they're not inherently wrong. It's a harsh way to label the functions we bring," Farrin explained.

"Right. My job is to ensure Atticus is thinking of himself. Pursuing goals, dreams, remembering to eat, remembering to do nothing. You know that kind of stuff. Self-care kind of stuff," Lude said proudly, his hands mounted to his hips as he stared off into the distance.

"That doesn't sound so bad," the Doctor said thoughtfully.

"Exactly! Thank you." Lude struck a pose in excitement towards the Doctor's recognition. "You hear that Farrin, it doesn't sound so bad. Why would eating be bad?" He boasted, glowing now that he finally had someone to back him up.

"Nothing, if you weren't trying to convince him to not waste his money when he could just steal it," Farrin his voice low as he crossed his arms.

"Details! I'm worried about Atticus eating. Not whether some yahoo decided to keep their baked goods accounted for or not." Lude mirrored Farrin, turning away from his comment.

"Right, that's my job," Farrin sighed.

"What a boring job." Lude smirked.

"If only."

*I see what they mean now. This is balance. A constant back and forth. A balance of give and take. The need to take care of myself first but doing so in a fashion that isn't wrong. This is the true struggle of light and dark. One isn't meant to conquer the other, they're just meant to keep balance.* The Doctor finally felt he was getting this straight.

"You got it!" Atticus gave the doctor a thumbs up.

"He got what?" Lude asked.

"The purpose of the light and dark persona," he replied happily, smiling with his eyes.

"Well, I'd hope so we just spent ages going over the entirety of this."

"Yes, but it can be confusing. Especially if you are approaching all this information with no knowledge of it. Imagine how Counticus must feel hearing all this 'world shattering' information. We basically just told him the life he thought he had was a farce and he's actually an artificial personality living inside the soul of a living being and he is not a doctor," Farrin reminded Lude, hoping it would help him apply a little empathy.

"Well . . . that's exactly what we told him." Atticus looked at the ceiling.

"Either way, now you are fully caught up on everything," Lude said with joy in his voice, happy this lengthy re-education phase was over.

"So, what's next then?" The Doctor asked.

"Aye? We just flippin told you," Lude grunted, returning to his annoyed stance as he slammed his palms on the table.

"With you fully loaded with the essences of the other persona the four of us will launch an assault against the nightmare and be rid of this riff raff once and for all," Farrin said with jubilation.

"Yes, let's go!" Lude roared as he elongated the word go in excitement.

"Okay!" Atticus chimed in.

"I suppose we no longer have any need for this place." As he said this, he moved his hand back and forth as if wiping up a mess and the area surrounding them cleared away. The Doctor's eyes widened as he watched the world around him disappear with wipe after wipe of Atticus' hand. While this happened Farrin was scribbling something down in a mini notebook and Lude was dancing around in excitement, making punching motions in front of him. This clearing of space had no effect on them. They didn't even react to it.

*Why would this be a surprise to them? This is the soul and mind of the true Atticus. The personas have the power to create and erase environments on a whim.*

"Right you are, Counticus," Atticus chirped as he finished clearing out the mess.

"Farrin, if you don't mind?"

"Not at all!" he said happily as he pocketed his book. He raised his hand above his head, paused a moment, and with a flick of his fingers produced a loud echoing snap that rang throughout the space around them. A cobblestone road rose from the emptiness.

"Come along," he said as he and Lude headed down the newly formed road.

"Where are we going?" the Doctor asked.

Atticus turned and took his hand.

"To the core of Atticus."

Lude threw his hand up, waving them to follow.

"Where the heart of Atticus sleeps," he said, lacing his hands behind his head as he walked on.

The group of four made their way down the cobblestone road. The final battle, in sight and the hope that the true Atticus will finally be freed of the evil embodiment they called the Nightmare.

# CHAPTER 11

They made their way down the cobblestone road. Their steps echoed throughout the world around them. Off in the distance the stones rose from the darkness forming a path for the party to follow. The road was wide enough that the group could have walked side by side in a row of four, but it was Lude and Farrin leading the way while Atticus and the Doctor walked side by side, hands still held.

The Doctor looked around the vast blackness surrounding them. Looking over the edge of the pathway the concept of never-ending deepness caused the Doctor to swallow in fear.

*Heh . . . one wrong step and you'd fall into oblivion . . . .* He gulped at the idea.

"Not really." Atticus replied.

Even after everything that had happened so far, this phenomenon still took the Doctor by surprise.

"Watch." Atticus instructed as he released the Doctor's hand and hopped out into the black void. His feet just hit the empty space devoid of noise.

"See?" He knelt and placed his hand *through* the empty space.

"It bends to whatever you're thinking," Atticus said.

"If you want to go down, you just go down." He stepped down like on a staircase.

"If you want to go up, you just go up." Atticus said, leaping back up and landing on the cobblestone path.

"How?"

Atticus giggled at the question.

"This isn't like the normal world you think you're familiar with. Here, things just . . . are what you want them to be. It's also one of the reasons the nightmare struggles moving around in this space."

The Doctor still struggled to understand what he meant.

"He is right, you know." Farrin's voice boomed throughout the space. From below he rose and grew bigger and bigger until he was a giant beside the road, his stomach now taking up space beside them.

Then Lude came falling from above and landed on the road before them.

"The heart, mind, soul it's all one massive, intertwined plane of existence. Everything can be and cannot be all at once."

Farrin looked down at the trio.

"We persona are born from this place and as such we have a strong understanding of the way it works." He shrank back into the darkness below. Once out of sight Farrin's voice could still be heard.

"What Atticus means; is we have a mastery of this place that no outsider could ever hope to understand. Not even the nightmare." Farrin appeared in front of him out of thin air, his body phasing into sight almost completely transparent until he was solid again.

"Yeah, and thanks to that knowledge we're able to do stuff like make 'hideaways' for stuff so we can keep it away from the nightmare. We hid the valley, we've hidden the Summit, the Core, all the important stuff. It's all hidden far away from the nightmare," Lude stated, his arms crossed, and eyes closed while he nodded.

"We did this to make its job harder."

"What job?" the Doctor asked.

The three looked at one another before replying to the Doctor.

"The nightmare's sole purpose is to corrupt," Lude said.

Farrin looked at the Doctor with a serious focus in his eyes.

"Its job is to absorb, or destroy, all the persona residing inside someone, make its way to the core, and corrupt the heart."

"If it succeeds, then there is no saving that living being," Atticus said softly.

"They're lost, with no way to create new persona. Their heart blackens and gives into the commands and orders of the nightmare."

"They just lose themselves?" The Doctor's eyes shook with dread as he asked.

"It's more than just losing yourself." Lude's voice was cold in his reply. His hand reached up to scratch the back of his head.

"If you lose yourself, it's usually from some kind of trauma. Your heart and mind can produce new persona to either establish a new you, or help you recover the old you. But this . . . " His eyes opened wide as he stared down the road into the blackness, as if he had just seen death.

Farrin placed a hand on Lude's shoulder offering him a touch of comfort. Lude looked at him, the sadness still in his eyes. He then quickly brushed his nose and shrugged Farrin's hand off as he turned away from the group.

Farrin took a deep breath and looked back at the Doctor.

"This is far worse. Your soul becomes trapped in your own body, the heart blackened and unable to let anything in but the nightmare. Your mind becomes clouded, and you can't think, can't hear, it becomes unable to understand anything but the word of the nightmare. You no longer have any control, and your soul becomes a permanent audience member to your body's actions. You can't control your words, your actions, your choices, or any decision. You simply are trapped watching this nightmare use your body as a vessel for destruction. Without the persona, your soul has nothing to help it. With the heart corrupted it is unable to create new persona. Your body becomes your tomb and overtime your soul just fades away from existence losing itself to the ever-devouring nightmare."

"Why can't it just outright go to the core?" the Doctor wondered.

*If the nightmare can do all of that . . . why waste time chasing down persona?*

"Ahh, amazing question. Theoretically it could, but it cannot access the heart. No matter how it might try to break down the doors it will never succeed so long as the persona are present," Farrin explained.

Atticus looked up at the Doctor.

"That's why I made you. To extract the essence of the other personas so that even if they're destroyed the door will remain shut." He smiled.

"But if I fall, doesn't that mean the door will open again?" the Doctor questioned, holding his hand to his chest where the essences slumbered, the warmth radiating into his palm.

"Technically no, but at this point maybe." Atticus shrugged not entirely knowing the answer.

"This is a unique instance, but should you be destroyed, the essence would return to their crystals. However, since Atticus used those as a decoy for the nightmare they are likely destroyed now. In which case, yes, those essence would simply return to the heart of Atticus and remove the seal protecting it."

The Doctor let out an audible gulp.

"But fear not," Farrin soothed as he gave him a smile, "Lude and I would also have to fall in order for it to remove the final seal."

Lude snorted at the notion.

"Yeah, and that isn't about to happen . . . at least not me. This old codger might kick the bucket, but me? Yeah right," he boasted as a cocky grin slid across his face.

Farrin rolled his eyes at his counterpart.

"The mind, the soul, and the heart are a mysterious entity to say the least. It is thanks to this complexity that the nightmare has struggled to completely overtake Atticus. As long as we remain, we won't let it win and take control." His smile made the Doctor feel a bit more at ease.

Farrin placed a reassuring hand on the Doctor's shoulder and the team continued down the cobblestone path. The world around them was devoid of any landscapes or vistas, but at random occasions images would appear. Some near the road, others further away. They'd light up and then fade as they walked on. Some of the images moved as if the event was happening right before them before fading out of existence again.

"These are the memories of Atticus," Farrin explained.

"Usually this place is more put together. Kind of like a big train hub or shopping district. You'd normally be able to just walk from place to place that had significance to Atticus." Lude's voice was thoughtful as he tried to describe the idea.

"And . . . it is not like that now because of the nightmare?" The Doctor turned his eyes to Lude.

Farrin raised his pointer finger happy to hear the Doctor was starting to follow along.

"A good idea! While the nightmare was the reason behind its removal, it was Lude and I who broke this hub into sections. Some were even completely hidden away."

"Yeah, like I said before. The nightmare doesn't understand how this place works. Even though it's been here for almost a decade it still doesn't understand the ins and outs of this place. That's why we broke it apart and hid them all over the place." Lude's voice coated in pride as he hit his fist against his chest.

"How did the nightmare find the valley then?" the Doctor questioned.

Lude puckered his lips and turned his gaze upwards, avoiding the question as he picked up speed and walked ahead of the group. Farrin gave a small chuckle.

"I see Lude is avoiding this one. It was because of Lude, Atticus, and me that it was able to find you. We kept journeying back and forth from the valley so, of course, it was only a matter of time before it picked up on where we were going. Because of that it picked up on the location and found you all."

"True. It was time to extract you anyway. You had finished absorbing the essence of the others a while ago. It's part of why the nightmare was able to reach you via your dreams. It was channeling the energies of the persona as it tried to hunt them down. I don't think it realized you were housing them all, at least, it didn't at the time of me throwing the crystals at it," Atticus recalled, his finger tapping against his cheek. "I wonder if that was the right move."

The group continued down the cobblestone path as memories of Atticus' life blipped in and out of existence around them, images of a smiling child to a roughed-up teenager with scratches on his arm. From swimming to stealing food. All was here to see as the childhood to adulthood played out around them like a living scrapbook.

**Diary Entry xx-11-xxxx**

It's been months since I left the company of the family.

I've been having these weird feelings lately.

For a while there it was as if I was really fighting myself inwards . . . like I couldn't decide who I was or what I wanted. But lately I've just felt devoid of anything.

I have no appetite.

I have no interests.

I've been moving from place to place doing anything to just try and feel something. Keeping myself on the road fighting off monsters, dealing with bandits, whatever crosses my path. While these things happen, it makes me feel for a moment. But once it's done . . . those feelings just go away. As if they've gone back to sleep. I'm chasing those feelings trying to get something, anything to stick for more than a second.

Before I left, I'd go back and forth with anger and regret. I would laugh, feel happy, enjoy a good meal and whatever else, but now I just feel lost. As if I don't know who I am anymore . . . I feel closed off even to myself. I think back to the words I heard as a kid

*Who are you?And what do you want?*

. . . but I just don't know . . . you know?

I don't know . . . I wish I could just find myself again . . .

I can't even remember who said that to me, but the words stayed, and I'd do anything to find my answers.

I want to know who I am.I want to know my purpose.I want to have a home, a place of peace. Of rest.

I want to go home.

# CHAPTER 12

A humming noise filled the space and suddenly words echoed loudly throughout the air around them. Words started to take physical shape and appear in the air, much like the images and memories did.

*Who am I?*

*What do I want?*

The words would come in random places of the darkness. They'd appear brightly when the words were heard, then fade and new words would appear as the next lines were spoken.

*I wish I could find myself again . . .*

The words I wish to find myself again repeated many times as the words appeared and disappeared around the group, then the words stopped, and the world was quiet once more.

"Poor thing," Farrin said, clearing his throat as his head angled upwards.

Lude started hitting his chest and clearing his throat in an effort to mask his feelings.

"Come on." His voice cracked as a tear ran down his cheek. He turned away from the group quickly to try to hide it.

The Doctor looked at the pair as they marched onwards.

*They're responding to the feelings of the true Atticus. They must feel his sorrow, that desperate plea to feel whole again. The sadness and loneliness that must be running rampant inside must be so overwhelming. How do they keep it together?* The Doctor's brows raised in sympathy as he contemplated how the two handled such a burden.

"Yes. Organic persona are extremely in tune with their living being. Lude and Farrin much more so than the others. They're the original persona, but I can feel it too." Atticus closed his eyes, placing his hand on his heart.

*But I don't . . .*

"Probably not. Artificial persona are not heavily impacted by the living being. It makes sense you are devoid of feelings about it. But, you're also a relatively new AP. In time you'll feel it too." Atticus comforted him with encouragement. It helped put the Doctor's worries at ease.

"Here we are." Farrin cupped his hands together behind his back as his feet landed firmly at the end of the long road.

The Doctor brought his attention to the front of the group. He knew they were at the end of the road, but aside from that, there was no indication anything was there. He looked beyond the road but nothing grabbed his attention as he scanned the horizon. The Doctor opened his mouth to say *"There's nothing here,"* but knew there was likely more to it. At this point he just closed his mouth and waited to see what would happen.

"All right, Lude, give me your hand," Farrin said as he held his out for Lude to take.

"Dude . . . " Lude was preparing to give Farrin attitude at the absurd request, but he remembered the reason for it.

"Fine," he dragged the word out in a groan. "But only because of all this," he waved his hands around before him as motioned about the void.

"Obviously," Farrin groaned in annoyance at the childish response.

The Doctor gave a smile at the pair. *Even in these dire times their nature is still to feud. To balance one another.*

They took one another's hand. Farrin's left and Lude's right. They both lowered their heads and closed their eyes. Farrin placed his right hand against his chest gently in a fist and Lude did the same with the left. They released their fists and laid their open hands against their own chest as their voices rang out. They started to sing a gentle and soothing song. It was a short melody, akin to a lullaby really, and on their third pass through of the song a bright light appeared in front of the pair. As the singing continued the light grew brighter and bigger until a mighty tower of light rose from the darkness. Their eyes opened now, focused on the massive structure before them. They raised their arms while the song continued. The final notes left their throats and silence fell upon their ears again and after a brief moment a loud chime, broke the silence and the light faded. In its place was a massive stone door.

The door appeared to be about twenty feet tall and ten feet wide. The stone was smooth and had a soft grey color. On the surface of the door was an etched picture of a man's sleeping face. Around the frame of the door were five grey crystals, and a white glass knob on the left and black glass knob on the right.

"This is what the nightmare is searching for?" the Doctor asked as he looked between each part of the door.

The others gave a nod.

"But why are we here? Couldn't it have just followed us here? We'd be delivering him to the core on a red carpet?" Worry added to the weight of his words.

"Yeah," Lude's voice was low in his reply.

"It should be here any minute, actually," Atticus stated as he looked at his wrist pretending to check the time.

"Yes, everything is falling into place." Farrin cleared his throat as prepared himself.

*What? Why would we lure it all the way here and what are we going to do about it when it does get here? Talk it out? This thing is hunting persona and right now we're all lumped together at the door to the heart of Atticus. We've just delivered every single component it needs to take control of Atticus.*

"That's true. Don't lose hope yet. We have a couple secret weapons up our sleeve." Atticus' calm and chipper tone helped the Doctor's rampant mind slow down.

It was odd to see what essentially appeared to be a child comforting an adult. In many ways though, it was the Doctor who was the child.

"WELL, WELL, WELL. LOOK WHAT WE HAVE HERE," a raspy growl crept into the space around the group.

"IF IT ISN'T FARRIN AND LUDE. HOW KIND OF YOU TO REVEAL THE CORE FOR ME." It's voice, enriched with excitement, coming from behind the group.

They all turned to the door to see the nightmare had perched itself atop it.

"Nightmare." Lude's voice dropped into a scratchy growl as his eyes landed on it.

"We wondered when you might show yourself," Farrin called out to it as he pointed at the monster.

"OH, I WASN'T FAR BEHIND." Its maniacal smile stretching ear-to-ear, white fangs glinting as he looked down at the group.

"We know. Your stench of rot and ruin wasn't exactly easy to miss," Atticus shouted up at the foul creature.

It's smile faded as his blood red eyes widened as he glared at the child.

You could cut the tension with a knife; everyone knew what was to come.

Lude hunched over as if ready to pounce, his fingers moving up and down to get his grip ready.

Farrin's demeanor was cool and collected as he stood staring down the foe above them.

Atticus had a mischievous expression as he eagerly watched all the pieces of his plan fall into place, an unusual demeanor for the typically happy and cheerful boy.

The Doctor gazed upward at the creature. The nightmare that had haunted his every dream and thought sat before him, his aura of malice stirring unease inside.

The nightmare looked down at the group. Across it's shoulder was the scythe. Gripped in his hand the weapon lightly bounced on it's shoulder waiting for the moment to be right.

"I'M GOING TO ENJOY CUTTING YOU TO PIECES, ATTI-CUS. THIS WILL FINALLY BE THE END OF YOU ALL AND THE TRUE ATTICUS WILL BE MINE AT LAST!" Its raspy low voice danced with excitement as it taunted the four.

The nightmare slowly rose to its feet. Its scythe resting on its shoulder, poised to strike at any moment.

The group took their positions, except for the Doctor who stood there watching, his pulse increasing at the sight of the nightmare readying itself. He thought back to the last encounters he had with this horrid creature.

"TODAY THE LIGHT AND DARK COME TO AN END! THIS TIME YOU WONT BE LEFT TO MEND!" It said hysterically. As its final words were spoken it phased out of their view.

"YOU DIE FIRST!" Its voice boomed around them.

When it phased back into view it had appeared behind Farrin, but he had already raised his hand to his shoulder, ready to counter. A loud clang rang out as the curved blade of the scythe came to a halt as a pure white steel longsword stopped its pursuit. The sword had intricate gold designs along the blade as well as designs etched into the center of the blade. The handle appeared gold as it twisted and turned from the blade to hilt spilling over to create a guard to protect his hand. Farrin pushed upwards, thrusting the blade of the scythe back above the nightmare and he turned around with a fast swing. The hum of the blade rang out around them as it cut through the air towards the nightmare. It leaned back into its heels pushing away in a dash to escape the counter of Farrin's attack.

"Dude, save some for me, man!" Lude's voice rang out in a gruff bark. Not wanting to be shown up by Farrin, Lude performed a cartwheel jump from his position over Farrin, bringing his orientation forward as he descended upon the nightmare, summoning a sword into his hands. A low grunt escaped him as he mustered strength into his arms, commanding the blade downwards with a heavy swing towards the creature. The nightmare, surprised by the attack, jumped back once again as soon as its foot had landed and evaded Farrin's initial counter. It narrowly dodged Lude's surprise attack. The nightmare's blood red eyes glowed with rage as its gaze locked onto the duo. Its feet landed hard. It leaned forward on the balls of its feet and lunged towards the pair, the scythe readied behind it for its lustful attack. Farrin and Lude took their fighting positions, blades ready.

"Divination's Light!" Atticus' voice called out from behind the pair.

The nightmare's feet stomped into the ground as it landed before them, and its scythe began its flight toward them but light quickly descended from above, enveloping the nightmare. The pressure of the light caused his scythe to stop. It let out a cry of pain as it stood, trapped within the light. The nightmare looked over its body in agony. Steam rose up from its arms, legs, and anywhere the light touched. The light's embrace was searing the creature. The intensity of the heat meant the nightmare could be set ablaze at any moment.

"Saint's Slash!" Farrin shouted, lashing towards the beast again, his blade glowing with pure light as it tore through the air and slashed through the chest of the nightmare. Darkness tore free of the beast as it roared in pain. Farrin hopped away after his attack connected and a fraction of a second later Lude came crashing down from the skies above.

"Darkness Fall!" Lude roared. The ground shook and splinted as his fist tore into it. The instant Lude landed, he phased out of sight. Reappearing, he crashed down onto the nightmare with his sword and vanished again. His assault continued until he phased away one last time, pausing high above the nightmare raising the hilt of his blade beside his face. He pointed the tip of the weapon at the nightmare, and the blade glowed with purple light.

"Ragnarok," Lude voice was smooth and calm now. A blaze of purple flames enveloped his body. The ball of purple fire fell with such speed and force the others had to throw their hands up to shield their eyes. The stone broke and pieces sent flying away as the orb smashed into the nightmare, destroying the road it stood on.

The creature was sent flying away. As the flames subsided, there stood Lude, sword resting against his shoulder. When he opened his eyes, they glowed with the same color and ferocity that the flames possessed. Farrin and Lude took their place in front of Atticus and the Doctor, blades readied for the next assault.

The nightmare growled in anger as it slammed its fist into the ground, and then lifted itself back to its feet. Snapping its fingers, the scenery around them changed from black void to a field and road. This was the same road that the true Atticus defeated those bandits on ages ago, a time when the nightmare influenced his actions and turned him into a bloodthirsty cutthroat.

It brushed itself off with a chuckle.

"NOT BAD, NOT BAD." It teased as it examined the tears in its own clothing, black and red liquid coursing beneath the garments.

"BUT WE'RE JUST GETTING STARTED HERE." It raised its left hand and let out a loud snap. As soon as it did the five persona appeared in the air above the nightmare, all gritted their teeth in rage at the group; their eyes devoured by blackness, faces stained with black tears rolling down their cheeks. Their hands clenched and opened as their nails had grown out into razor sharp claws. Hissing and growling while snapping their jaws, teeth stretching into long fangs, as they stared at the group ready to attack at any moment.

Atticus' mouth hung open at the display and the Doctor staggered backwards in shock to see his patients in such a horrific state.

"What have you done to them?" he cried out in horror.

"WITHOUT THEIR ESSENSE TO KEEP THEM SANE, I DE-CIDED TO DO A LITTLE RESTRUCTURING." The nightmare laughed, pleased with the disgust they expressed. "DEVOUR THIS FOOL, MY PETS!" It commanded pointing its scythe towards the Doctor.

They all lunged towards him, Tristan landed on the ground and rushed at him like a dog on his hands and feet. Rex and Abbey descended towards him in the air approaching as a pair. They wrenched back a hand, opposite from one another, claws ready to slash through him. Davis and Sarah landed on the ground and sprinted toward him with their hands stretched open, claws curved, thirsty for his flesh. Farrin and Lude both attempted to rush to his aid but as they turned to do so, the swing of the nightmare's scythe came down before them. Caught off guard, the pair staggered backwards as their anger-filled gazes turned to see the vibrant red eyes laughing back at them.

The nightmare's monstrous grin taunting them.

"TSK TSK. YOU DIDN'T FORGET ABOUT ME, DID YOU, BOYS?" It's deep voice teased as it made itself the wall between them and their friends.

# CHAPTER 13

Atticus saw the two were cut off and attempted to create a barrier to keep the fallen persona away. Clear hexagonal shapes stacked together from the ground up into the sky creating a wall to prevent their path forward. Unfortunately, Atticus wasn't fast enough, and Rex and Abbey slipped over the top of the barrier before it could be finished. The Doctor crossed his arms in front of him as Abbey and Rex's feet crunched into the ground and slid towards him. Both thrust their fists into his arms, the force sending him soaring backwards. His arms broke loose of their protective position as his back collided into the stone door. The force caused his arms to slam down against the door, his palms slapping the cold stone. The blow left his body locked against the door for a moment before gravity sent him to the ground with a heavy thud.

As his body lay slumped on the ground and his vision blurry, he could just barely see Abbey and Rex stomping towards him. Their teeth gnashing in excitement as their prey lay helpless before them. Atticus called out to the Doctor, but the force of the fallen persona crashed against the wall, forcing him to stay focused on keeping the wall up or else. Sadly, he couldn't go to his friend's aid and watched in fear as they continued to the Doctor.

"Get up, Counticus!" Lude commanded.

Farrin paused, holding his fist in front of his chest. It began to emit a glow with white and soft lime green colors, but the hum of the scythe broke his focus and his eyes jetted open, leaning backwards to dodge the nightmare's scythe once more.

"I DON'T THINK SO, OLD MAN!" It bellowed as it took multiple wide and heavy swings towards Farrin.

Lude bent his knees and launched himself into the sky. He hoped to get over Farrin and make it to the Doctor, but his flight was cut short as the nightmare's scythe came swirling up past the front of his body. Caught off guard, he instinctively flipped his body backwards away from the attack sending him falling head over heels to the ground below. Just before he was about to crash into the ground, he flipped his feet back under him, skidding into the earth. Rocks broke free from the forceful impact, dust grinding up and lingering in the air around him.

"Do you fucking mind?" Lude yelled at the nightmare, teeth clenched in anger as he raised a fist in anger.

"AS A MATTER OF FACT, I DO!" It laughed as a second scythe was collected. The nightmare, now wielding a scythe in each hand pursued, Lude and Farrin simultaneously.

A warmth enveloped the Doctor and his vision returned. When he looked down to his chest, he saw his own hand aglow with white and green light stretching out across his body. As the lights traced over his arms, hands, and the rest of him, he breathed a sigh of relief as the comforting warmth of the light enveloped him.

*Am I doing this?*

Abbey and Rex had stopped coming towards him and froze, shielding their eyes in pain as a bright light flooded out from behind the Doctor. He turned to see that the five essences had left his body and were placing themselves into the different crystals in the door. Each crystal lit up brilliantly, their shining light spilling out before the door. It caused the fallen persona to falter in their pursuits as they attempted to shield themselves from the light's radiance. The two remained frozen, almost petrified, unable to move. The light then returned to the crystals. Each pushed out a focused beam of colored light onto the Doctor.

*My head . . . it feels like it's . . . on . . . fire!* His mind screamed as the colored spotlights illuminated him, flooded with images, words, experiences, and memories as the pressure in his head grew. The lock Atticus had put in place to seal the Doctor's memories was being opened. Everything flooded back to him. In an overwhelming flurry he remembered his creation by Atticus, his own purpose. His head jerked back and his eyes glowed white.

> *You are to house the persona who will*
> *one day fall to the nightmare.Y*
> *ou will be our secret weapon.*
> *Counticus, I give you life as the ninth persona.*
> *You will guard the true Atticus at all costs regardless of what*
> *should befall the rest of us.*
> *I give you life as the Requiem Persona.*

With the seal broken, memories of the true Atticus rushed into his mind like a raging torrent of water, the pressure causing him to clench his head in pain. *This is too much . . . .*

As the lights faded, Rex and Abbey broke free of their displacement and rushed towards him once more. Memories still rushing through Counticus and his peripheral vision was blinded with white light, but despite that he sensed the two approaching. He drew back his right hand, while still grasping his head in his left, and swung his arm towards them. He heard them let out a groan of pain. Counticus opened one of his eyes and discovered he was wielding a large lance. Opening his other eye, he turned his focus to see the outcome of the monstrous pair of persona. All he saw was flecks of glittering colors as they evaporated upwards glimmering and fading from sight.

"Atticus!" he called.

Atticus perked up, head turning slightly towards the commanding call of his name, his hands trembling as kept the barrier up.

"Let the barrier fall," he commanded, with knees bent he built up strength. He lunged himself towards the barrier, fervor surging through his body. His eyes narrowed  locking his sights on the fallen person as he closed in on the wall.

*I remember who I am.*

The distinct glow of the hexagons became dim and before they could disappear, Counticus smashed through the remainder of the gate, his lance in hand plunging through the chests of Davis and Sarah as he soared past the other fallen persona. They too popped into thousands of speckled, glimmering lights before fading. Counticus widened his eyes at a space before him and the earth tore free climbing upwards producing a thick wall that he could catch himself on. His body somersaulted to change positions, landing on the wall as he turned around on the balls of his feet and launched himself once more, this time ascending skyward. The force of his jump shook through the newly produced wall and it crumbled.

A smile stretched across Atticus' face as he watched the display of Counticus' newly discovered abilities.

"WHAT?" The nightmare shouted seeing, Counticus take to the skies above.

"Well done, lad!" Farrin rejoiced, continuing his assault in order to draw back his foe's attention.

"Let's fucking go!" Lude rallied, slapping his free hand against his upper thigh. "I don't even need this!" he mocked as he threw his sword behind him. It disappeared as it left his grasp. Lude glided across the ground with blinding speed. He drew his fist back and thrust it hard into the ribs of the unaware nightmare.

A loud boom erupted as the nightmare was sent lurching backwards away from Farrin, its body spinning through the air, end over end, before bouncing and sliding against the ground, sending dust and rock flying everywhere.

∽

Counticus saw Lude lunge for the nightmare and as his punch sent the nightmare off, Counticus redirected his flight back to the ground below. The wind ripped past his ears as he accelerated to the ground. He grasped his lance with both hands, now holding it outwards in front of him, guiding his path down. Just before hitting the ground, he flung his feet under him while repositioning his hands on the lance. As he came to the ground, Tristan dodged his assault. With a loud slam and crunch, Counticus crashed into the earth, the ground giving and breaking under his feet. He used the remaining momentum to give a strong hop backwards from the debris onto solid ground. The earth where Tristan once stood collapsed into itself.

Tristan rushed towards him, his claws opened, ready to slash. Counticus closed his eyes as the fallen persona continued for him.

"Sorry, lad," he said solemnly as he sidestepped the forceful attack and countered with a pinwheel spin of his lance which cut through the boy, exploding him into a spectacle of glinting color.

With that, the fallen persona had been dealt with and Atticus ran to the side of Counticus.

"We did it!" he cheered, jumping into the air, his hand poised for a high five.

Counticus smirked and held up his hand up. "Hell yeah."

A clap echoed through the air as a small celebration for their efforts. When a spectacle of purple and white light ruptured in the skies above, they craned their heads to look upwards and watch.

❧

Farrin looked over to see Counticus deliver the massive jump attack to the fallen persona.

"Very good, Counticus, leave the nightmare to us," he said, proud to see how well they were doing.

"Lude, it's time."

"Yeah, all right. Team attack, let's go!" he said, rubbing his hands together.

The pair ascended into the air hand in hand. Farrin's right locked with Lude's left hand. Each emitting, an almost blinding, glow. Farrin's was, of course, white, while Lude's was a deep purple. They turned to face one another and cupped their hands in each others. As they closed their eyes the pair started to spin in a circular motion. Faster and faster they began their torrent turned on its side still accelerating.

"Ying and Yang's Promise!" their voices exclaimed as they spun faster until they were simply a blur of white and black. The nightmare lifted its body back onto its hands and then rose to its feet. As it stood up, it looked up to see that the fallen persona were gone. Lude and Farrin launched another attack, and Atticus just gave Counticus a high five.

"WAIT A SECOND," The nightmare coughing as it tried to speak.

It noticed the crystals surrounding the door had all been lit and the colored aura surrounding 'the Doctor' was that of the fallen persona.

"SO, THAT'S HOW YOU LOT WANT TO PLAY IT, EH?" His face stretched wide with an evil smile, and he began laughing hysterically. "WHY DIDN'T I SEE IT BEFORE!?"

The nightmare opened a black void below him and started to fall into it when the skies above opened and unleashed an otherworldly beam of light. Balanced with the powers of both light and darkness, this massive beam of twin counterpart energy plunged towards the nightmare below. Both the nightmare and the beam were swallowed into the newly made void.

This beam ran for a full minute before Lude and Farrin finally slowed their spinning. As their attack came to a halt, the pair released hands, returned their orientation to normal, and they both planted their feet firmly onto the ground. The beam that had torn through the sky dwindled until it was no more.

Both stood there in silence as Atticus, in the distance, ran towards them, waving his arm above his head as he approached.

" . . . .I hate that attack," Lude said, his vision spinning.

" . . . A powerful one though . . . but . . . it is a doozy." Farrin burped as he placed his fist against his lips.

The sound of Farrin made Lude's stomach turn and he placed his arms over his stomach.

"Don't say . . . doozy . . . " he spit and groaned painfully.

"Why?"

"Because it's lame." Lude groaned out.

"You're lame."

"Ugh, I want to barf." Lude took in a deep breath, panting, as his body tried to recover from their joint efforts.

"Great job, guys!" Atticus exclaimed with glee as he finally reached them. "Oh, you guys okay though? You both look sick."

Lude stood straight, crossing his arms.

"Obviously, I'm fine." His body swayed as he tried to force his balance to be straight. His eyes ticked left and right not being able to focus on a single point yet.

Atticus let out a laugh as he watched.

"We did it though, guys! We actually beat the nightmare!" he cheered.

Both Lude and Farrin smiled wearily, exhausted from the aftereffects of their joint attack.

"That we did lad. That we did." Farrin placed a hand upon Atticus' head. "We couldn't have done it without you two," he said, looking down at the boy. His eyes then turning upwards to look at Counticus in the distance.

Counticus was still standing in the remains of his own intense battle. He raised a hand in acknowledgement of their efforts.

Farrin saw Counticus give a wave and in turn he and Lude both raised their hands to wave back.

As they did, two small black twirling voids opened on the ground behind Lude and Farrin. Out of each void a long, thick, black tentacle emerged. Each positioned its tip towards Farrin and Lude, hardening the end like steel, and thrust towards them. Each tentacle plunged through the soft of their necks, just below their skulls, and pierced through the front of their faces. The pair stood frozen for a moment, their eyes wide from the sudden foreign object struck through them. The tentacles retracted themselves from their heads and back through the void. Farrin and Lude's bodies fell lifeless to the ground. Atticus' once smiling face was replaced with one of horror as he watched his friends' eyes go vacant.

"GOTCHA!" the nightmare's voice roared through the, once joyous, celebration.

"No!" Atticus screeched out in agony.

Another void opened, similar in height to a door, behind Atticus and out walked the nightmare, laughing as it clapped, taunting their efforts with mock acknowledgements. Atticus turned to confront his enemy, but he was met with a swift boot to his body. The force sent him flying backwards past the lifeless bodies of Farrin and Lude.

*Atticus!* Counticus shouted internally as he ran to his friend.

Atticus hoisted himself from the ground to his knees, hands pressing into the dirt, coughing as he gasped for air. He looked up again to face the nightmare now bent down beside him.

"TSK TSK TSK. POOR ATTICUS. NO ONE LEFT TO SAVE YOU NOW, HMM?" it taunted the boy as he pointed to the corpses of Farrin and Lude with his thumb, their essence having begun to float above their bodies.

"N-no . . . " Atticus coughed as he clenched his shirt, still trying to recover from the blow.

Counticus, not wanting to waste more time, leapt over Farrin and Lude.

"Are you two really going to let this be the end of you? Death by nightmare octopus tentacles?" he grunted to the essences.

The nightmare hadn't forgotten about Counticus and he wasn't surprised to see him finally approaching. What did take him by surprise was the essences he had just freed from the Farrin and Lude started to return to their bodies.

"NO. NO. NO NO NO NO!" the nightmare shouted, shoving Atticus back into the ground. It ran towards them again. "WHAT DID YOU DO REQUIEM!?"

It growled in confusion at Counticus.

Counticus dug his heels into the ground and leaped towards the nightmare. He grabbed it by the collar and dragged it back near Atticus. As his feet slid into the ground, he hurled the nightmare away from them. The nightmare caught itself on its hands and feet and rose again. It glared in anger at Counticus as it ran towards them.

"I'VE HAD ENOUGH!" It slapped its hands together and when it pulled them apart, it's scythe appeared once more. Grasping it from the air it pulled its arms back reading its attack. "IT'S TIME THAT YOU AND I TOOK THIS MORE SERIOUSLY."

Its raspy voice growled.

It stopped a short way from Atticus and Counticus and began to spin the weapon faster and faster, the scythe glinting light off its blade, so fast it created the image of a rotating blade. It then slammed the blade of the scythe into its own chest. Its head jerked backwards, and its mouth tore at the corners, up through its cheeks, until finally its jaw broke and tore itself in half. The sound of breaking bone and tearing flesh ripped through the air. It's body convulsed as it fell to the floor. Bones continued to break, and black and red blood shot out of the pile as it moved and pulsed. When suddenly from the pile emerged a massive fleshy and bulbous creature. Twin arms emerged from the pile, long in length but veiny and wide at the hands, the fingers slapped and swayed around and were long tentacles. A long, thin neck emerged from the pile next, and a rag doll-like head came into view. It had a gaping mouth with a long snake-like tongue, its eyes large and bulging outwards. It's tiny pupils lurching in different directions. Bags under its eyes hung low exposing the fleshy part of the eye below it. Sharp spear-like teeth jetted out from the mouth, and finally its bulbous body emerged from the pile bringing its appearance to fruition.

Atticus collapsed to the ground, watching as this monstrosity came into existence. He stared with no words, only fear. Sweat ran down his face.

A firm grasp of his shoulder came, and he looked up to see Counticus.

"Don't worry, I'm with you," he said.

"All my memories are back now, and the essences of the fallen persona are with me."

Atticus looked behind Counticus and saw the faint trails of light, almost as if trying to hide, wisping its way towards Counticus. The light came from the crystals embedded in the door now resonating with Counticus.

"Weapon change!" Counticus called out. His lance suddenly vanished, and the clothes he was wearing changed too. He was now wearing metal shoulder pads, padded armor, boots of leather with metal atop them and fur on each piece, thick gloves wrapped around his forearm and hands. In his hand he now carried an axe with massive crescent moon-like blades on each side of the pole and the entire weapon was made of cool grey steel.

"You do remember!" Atticus exclaimed.

"Yes. The true Atticus is a master of weapons, which means we are too." His face was hard and bold as he stared down the newly formed nightmare.

Atticus rose to his feet once more.

"I've got your back," he called out. "Let's finish this!"

"Let's." Counticus echoed as they stood ready before the grotesque beast.

# CHAPTER 14

"YOUR HOPE ENDS HERE AND YOUR MEANINGLESS EX-
ISTENCE WITH IT!" the beast's voice tore through the air, altered,
distorted, and demonic by its new form. It raised both its hands overhead before slamming them into the ground at the pair.

Counticus grabbed Atticus' arm and started running away from the
attack, but the force of the slam still caught them shaken and off
balance, the two staggered on the quaking earth. Counticus noticed
a sudden change in the air. He looked over his left shoulder and saw
some of the finger tentacles rushing towards him. He tossed Atticus in
front of him as gently as he could while turning to face the assault. He
gripped his axe and swung it upwards, mustering forth as much power
as he could. The axe let out a low twang as its blade sliced through
the tentacles with ease. Dark liquid sprayed from the severed ends
while the beast let out a piercing screech. The tentacles let out a loud
squash as it fell hard against the ground. Writhing on the floor, dark
liquid gushed forth from the wound. The nightmare's large ogling
eyes turned red with anger as it fixed Counticus in its sights.

Counticus re-positioned himself, sensing another attack coming.

"Look out!" Atticus yelled as he pointed at the earth below them.

The ground was marked with a black thorned pattern that emitted a
grey glow, growing brighter by the second.

The hiding colors intensify as they wisped their way over to Counticus once more.

"Weapon change!" he called out again and the colors brightened at the command.

His armor started fading away, returning to his previous attire. His axe burst with light and reshaped back into the lance he had before and the colors surrounding him retreated once more back to their crystals. Once the lance appeared, Counticus performed a backflip, the force jumping him away from their position. Flipping away from the attack, he grabbed Atticus by the arm and dragged him skyward. As they soared out of range of the marks , the paterns detonated, and an explosion raged through the spot. Rubble launched from the earth as dust polluted the air and the nightmare let out a roar when it realized it had missed its mark. Twice.

Atticus looked up at Counticus with concern.

"We'll be alright," Counticus offered and he stood ready as he took his place in front of Atticus.

The beast roared as its body flared its limbs upward.

As the creature's roar echoed throughout the battlefield dark spheres appeared in the sky. Their color was a gradient from black to purple while their cores had a pure white hue. The hundreds of spheres slowly descend on the arena. One reached the ground and as it made contact it exploded in a column of purple light and lightning.

*Great. Not only are these everywhere, but when they go off, they leave a wide radius of attack.* Counticus looked back at Atticus. Atticus met his eyes, the feeling of determination mirrored in Counticus' eyes.

"I'll be okay, you go." Atticus' words tried to match the confidence he received a moment ago, but his voice shook with fear.

Counticus rested a hand on the boy's head and gave him a smile.

"I'll be right back." he said before performing another powerful jump toward the nightmare.

As the spheres descended upon Atticus, he cast another barrier spell, but this time only raising it around himself. Soft blue and white hexagons appeared creating a dome of protective light once more.

The wind whipped past Counticus' ears as he soared above the ground in his pursuit of the nightmare. He kept his gaze on the beast while tracking the descending orbs. As they hit the ground and went off, Counticus turned his body left and right to maneuver around the explosions. One after another the orbs exploded with dark pulsing lighting. Counticus was able to get around them with ease. On the ground he spotted small voids and out from them slithered more long tentacles.

*Damn it.* Counticus pulled his legs forward to stop his momentum, effectively dropping him in the middle of the minefield of descending orbs. The tentacles launched simultaneously at him. He was able to sidestep the attacks as they rushed past him. He took the opportunity to slash his lance through them. With five, loud wet sounding squashes, the tentacles crashed into the earth before Counticus, gushing out dark liquid. The limbs retreated back into the voids. While his gaze was fixed on the retreating appendages his peripheral vision saw orbs fall just above him. The color from the crystals tried to wisp their way to him, their colorful stream stretched across the battlefield, jerking and jetting around orbs, but they could not make it in time and as the blasts began, they retreated to their crystals. Counticus had braced himself for the impact as he tried to back away, doing anything he could to put distance between himself and these attacks.

One hit the ground causing the pulsing lightning to pop and rise upwards. As the pulse widened it pushed hard against Counticus, knocking him backwards as the electricity ran though this body. He let out a grunt at the painful connection. This happened a second time. A third, and fourth . . . and fifth. He was trapped as the orbs fell upon him without signs of ending.

The nightmare let out a deafening roar of enjoyment as he found Counticus trapped in his attack and so it took this opportunity to send its tentacles in once more. Fixed on his body, the tentacles lunged with greater speed hoping to impale him like it had Farrin and Lude.

*This isn't good . . . I can't get out of here.* He looked around trying to find a way to escape. A loud hum rang into his ear when he looked down to see Atticus pop out of an orb of light that had suddenly appeared by his feet.

"Atticus!" he exclaimed as his eyes widened with concern.

"Promise Land!" Atticus called out as he held his hand up in front of him.

A blue wave burst out from behind them and rushed out onto the field in every direction. As it moved its way through the broken earth, wildflowers and grass grew anywhere the wave touched. A blinding blue and white light created a dome of energy over the pair and Counticus' body shimmered with light. The flowers raised their petals up to the sky and from them yellow light beamed upwards at each of the orbs causing them to explode far from the ground.

*My wounds … are healed?* Counticus dropped his guard and examined himself.

Atticus gave him a smile and gave his arm a gentle smack with his hand.

"Back to work!" Atticus said.

He nodded with appreciation as his eyes returned back to the nightmare.

From where they stood a large field of flowers was born and the skies opened to reveal a clear blue sunny day. Outside the circle dark clouds flooded the skies, rumbling with lighting and the earth lay barren and broken from the fighting. The beast seized the opportunity to attack. A small void opened behind Atticus. As the tentacle shot upwards with the intention of ending the boy, Counticus' hand tightly took hold of the tentacle, preventing its plan from playing out. It pulled and tugged, trying to wriggle itself free from the grasp. He plunged the tip of his lance into the grass beside him as he grasped the tentacle with his other hand. Pulling in opposite directions, he tore the tentacle in half and roars of pain poured out from the other side of the battlefield. He threw the dismembered tentacles to the ground and jumped towards the nightmare again, lance in hand.

The colors streamed out from the door to meet Counticus at his intended landing position in front of the nightmare. As his feet hit the ground, he slid forward as the colors twirled around his body and limbs once more. His attire returned to the armor and axe and then he took heavy swings at the beast. With each swing the axe cleaved through its discolored flesh, heaving off chunks from its body, the pieces making a wet squash into the ground beneath it. Counticus' axe showed no signs of stopping as it dismembered tentacle after tentacle. Dark liquid sprayed from severed limbs and body as it continued to be carved and butchered by Counticus. With a leap he slammed his axe through the right hand, severing it from the nightmare and the large body part plummeted into the ground. It let out another loud roar while dozens of tentacle emerged from the new crevasses of Counticus attack,. Flailing and swatting, a few managed to connect with the warrior's body, and launched Counticus away with a fierce thwap. The attack crushed his armor and left him without breath as his body flew through air. He tried to clench his abdomen where the pain radiated behind the broken armor.

The colors from the door flew once more to the man, enveloping him in light again. His broken armor faded, and the lance returned to his hand. He looked behind himself to see dozens of tentacles waiting to receive him with their piercing tips at the ready. He looked at the ground and slammed the tip of the lance into the earth causing him to come to a stop after a few feet. Once his momentum stopped, he jumped skyward. In anger, the creature launched its many limbs at the platform, smashing it to pieces while others chased Counticus into the sky. He turned his body to face them, stopping his trajectory and meeting the tentacles with a swing of his lance. After lobbing off the pursuing appendages he started to fall. Atticus mumbled something, but he was too far away to hear him. The ground was fast approaching when Counticus felt his velocity slowed to a crawl before stopping altogether. Wings sprouted from his shoes, keeping him afloat as he fended off the unending assault of the tentacles. He looked towards Atticus who shot him a thumbs up.

*This kid.* Counticus smirked.

Looking at the ground again, Counticus summoned up a pillar towards himself, his feet landing gently on the newly made stone. He fought back the remaining tentacles as the wings faded from his shoes. He swung over and over as the blade of the lance sliced through the tentacles. Cleaving off the ends, the remaining tentacles retracted themselves back through the voids.

"I've had enough of this," Counticus grunted as he pointed the tip of his lance at the nightmare.

His legs pulsed with purple and blue energy and clenched with strength as he summoned forth a momentous amount of power and launched himself into the air. Wind rushed through his hair, his eyes focused above as climbed through the clouds. This was the highest he had taken his jumps so far. Lightning cracked around him, bolts zipped by his body until he finally broke free from their pollution. On the other side was a starry night sky.

*Wasn't this day-light a moment ago?* He soon remembered he had changed the setting. He, as a persona, changed the environment to his will. *I can do this.*

He saw the parting in the clouds where Atticus' skill had created an opening, his eyes returning to the clouds below him. He heard a roar and his eyes widened as if they locked on to the exact position of the nightmare.

"Starfall!" he shouted as his body immediately lunged downwards, the lance guiding his descent. The strength of his fall pushed aside the clouds and created a tunnel as he traveled through them. In a flash of lighting Counticus' lance punctured through the body of the nightmare driving himself and the weapon straight through the beast's body. He leapt back out of the beast and onto the earth a short distance from it. Dark liquid gushed from where Counticus had entered, a geyser flowing upwards and raining down black and red liquid onto the defeated corpse. The body of the creature deflated and sprawled out like a broken heap of bones and flesh.

*Finally.*

The pile of flesh convulsed and quivered. From it emerged the shape of a man. It was simply a silhouette of the nightmare's original form, but instead of being black, its body was littered with stars and galaxies as if looking into the night sky. Its eyes opened and were simply pure white eye sockets. Long rigid, wire-like wings jetted out from its back. The ground trembled and quaked. Suddenly a roaring overtook Counticus' ears as the beast launched itself, crashing through Counticus as if he was no more an obstacle than a pile of leaves. The ground broke, leaving a crater in the earth where the nightmare had been standing, obliterating any remaining flesh left behind by its previous form. As Counticus was left dazed on the ground, the nightmare turned its gaze at Atticus, and in the next moment it was in pursuit.

ATTICUS!

The voice was pure, agitated, malicious and it left Atticus paralyzed in fear as its voice boomed all around him and Counticus.

Atticus flinched in pain, momentarily dropping his guard and before he could react, the nightmare's body was coming to tear through him. There was no time to react, nothing could be done, and so Atticus closed his eyes and stood tall, knowing his time had come. He would meet his end just as he foresaw it long ago.

As the nightmare reached the boy, an explosion of sound roared out before Atticus. The sound of rocks or metal grinding together lashed out from beneath the dust cloud that had formed, and as it started to settle Atticus saw two figures before him. It was Farrin and Lude. Their essence taking human shape, hands before them as their colored essence jetted outwards holding back the nightmare's attack.

"Farrin, Lude, you're alive!" Tears appeared in his eyes.

They gave him a warm smile and nodded.

"Atticus, you know what to do," Farrin's mouth did not move, but his words were heard all around.

Atticus nodded to the pair.

"It's time," his voice said grimly.

"Sorry kid . . . there's just no other way," Lude said, his voice apologetic.

"We believe in you."

Atticus smiled at the ground and nodded towards them. Their gaze returned to the nightmare.

Atticus cupped his hands together in prayer and his body popped into shimmering white light, the light rushing to cover the door to the heart of Atticus.

"Atticus!" Counticus shouted, his hand gripping the side of his head, still recovering from the nightmare's voice.

*It's okay, Counticus.*
*I always knew this day would come.*

"What do you mean?" His voice wavered.

*I, like you, have a role to fulfill.*

His light shined brightly around the door, and when it was fully absorbed into the rock the once sleeping face's eyes opened revealing bright white orbs.

*I will act as the final seal to protect Atticus.*
*Use this when the time comes.*

A small bead of light appeared before Counticus and from it a necklace emerged.

*When this is finished, return to the door.*
*This will show you the final memories you'll need.*

The voice of Atticus vanished.

Counticus looked down at the charm. Tears welled up and dropped onto the necklace. As the tears collided with it, a small chime echoed forth. He stood up to his feet once more and placed the charm around his neck.

"Don't worry, Atticus, I'll keep him safe." He wiped the remaining tears away with his palm. Counticus glared at the nightmare, his gaze piercing, and then, he rushed towards the creature.

Counticus swung downwards smashing it free of Lude and Farrin's barrier. The creature now found its back and wings embedded into the earth. The essences of Lude and Farrin rushed to Counticus.

"Our essences can't handle this anymore." Farrin stated.

"So, we're leaving this up to you, boss." Lude said.

"Don't let us down now."

Counticus nodded in acknowledgement.

"This is the last thing we can do." Farrin said as his ethereal body wound and shifted itself into the shape of the sword he used in the previous fight.

"Take this, the Griffin Blade, a divine blade meant to bring justice."

Counticus reached out to accept the blade. It's grip was warm to the touch.

"Oi, what the hell man!"

Lude scoffed, not wanting to be outdone by Farrin he too transformed into a blade, though a blade of darkness. A sword of pure black. It was a long, easy to swing blade with large spike-like adornments stretching out from the back of the blade that pulsed with purple embers.

"I named this Ragnarok. A blade meant to bring about the end. Use it to end this chump once and for all, all right?"

The blade of darkness was just the opposite of Farrin's, very cool to the touch, but the blade pulsed with so much fervor, tenacity radiating throughout his palm. Holding the blade made him feel capable of any task.

"Thank you," his voice lifted, genuinely grateful to the pair.

Farrin and Lude's bodies slowly became more and more transparent. Their physical bodies slowly drifting away.

*While Atticus might be the final seal, we are the second seal.* Farrin's voice spoke into his mind.

*Yeah, so when that day does come, you'll need us to unlock the door.* Lude added.

*Oh, but do remember we unlock the opposite.*

*Right so I unlock the old man's side.*

The sound of Farrin sighing came into Counticus' mind.

*And I unlocked the child's. Don't forget.*

*Seriously.* Counticus imagined Lude glaring at him down a pointed finger.

"I got it." He reassured them.

The blades let out a low glow acknowledging his words.

*We believe in you too, Counticus.* Lude's words sending warmth throughout Counticus

*See that our boy is kept safe.*

With their final words shared, their essences sifted into their respective blade.

The earth broke apart and from the rubble rose the nightmare once more, its empty white eyes fixed on Counticus. It lunged for its final assault.

The crystals from the door shined brightly as they launched outwards enveloping Counticus.

His eyes closed and opened once more.

"Weapon change," he called out.

His eyes changed to a bright blue.He now wore the jacket Lude had worn.White gloves appeared on his hands and cloth wrapping up his forearms like Farrin had.A white vest and tie replaced his shirt.In his hands he dual wielded the Griffon Blade in his right and the Ragnarok in his left.

Counticus was complete, and his final task realized as Requiem. He now housed all the powers of the persona before him.

*I'll use these powers to see you finished. In the name of Atticus, in the name of the fallen persona, I will cut you down.*

He ran toward the approaching nightmare. Griffon blade resting on his shoulder and his left arm pulled across the front of his body, as if to hug himself, embraced Ragnarok. As the two approached one another on a collision course, Counticus planted his feet firmly as he swung Ragnarok against the nightmare to parry its attack. Knocking it off center, he quickly slashed the Griffon blade downward making contact against the beast. In a flurry he swung his blades slashing through the nightmare one after the other. Following up the attacks he started swinging the blades together in joint hits, one after the other, cleaving against the crystalized body of the nightmare.

NO . . .

HOW?

HOW!?

The nightmare cried out but Counticus did not stop his flurry of blows against the beast. His body was engulfed in a mixture of white and purple flames as he brought both blades overhead and made one final strike through the nightmare leaving a deep x pattern broken into its crystal body. It glowed brightly before its body exploded and shattered. Parts of the crystalized body clamored against the ground, crystal shards spilling out and filling the barren battlefield, the pieces slowly started to evaporate.

Counticus watched as the remnants of the nightmare faded away. The sight was almost beautiful. Before he could take another breath in celebration of the end, one of the fragments started to bend and mold itself. As a liquid drop of the nightmare, it bent its small raindrop-like body towards Counticus.

I'LL BE BACK TO FINISH THIS, COUNTICUS. I'LL ALWAYS COME BACK! JUST YOU WAIT! THIS ISN'T OVER!

Counticus tried to stomp it out of existence, but it had slipped into the earth and disappeared. The battlefield vanished and Counticus found himself once again on the cobblestone road standing before the door to the heart of Atticus.

The eyes were open, pulsing white with the essence of Atticus, the colored crystals shining in brilliance. The two knobs remained empty and dormant. Counticus dismissed the blades of Farrin and Lude and as they faded, he noticed now that he wore a bracelet on each wrist. Inside was a small gem, that glowed white on the right, and black on the left.

"I did it . . . . no . . . " He stopped realizing he misspoke, "We did it." He meant the words to sound happy, but they were solemn. Now that the fight was over his body hunched a bit and sadness washed over Counticus as he realized what it cost to defeat the nightmare.

*Tristan.*
*Rex.*
*Abbey.*
*Davis.*
*Sarah.*
*Farrin.*
*Lude.*
*Atticus.*

*They all sacrificed themselves in order to protect the true Atticus. Your sacrifice will not go in vain my friends. I promise to keep these keys safe, to keep him safe.*

He held his hand outwards towards the door calling back the persona who slept there and the essences left their crystal slumber to reside within Counticus, his chest warm with their embrace.

*I'll keep you safe with me.* He placed his fist against his chest.

The crystals around the door lost their color and turned grey, and the white eyes began to slump as they closed, ready to sleep again.

*Come, Counticus. The battle is won today.*
*It is time to pass my final memories to you.*
*That you can fulfill your duty that we've entrusted to you.*

Counticus approached the door, the remaining white of the orbs glowing with a soft and gentle light. He placed his hand upon the stone. It was warm, just like he was. Counticus closed his eyes, the world going dark around him as he softly placed his forehead against the door. When he opened his eyes again, he found himself in a white void, but he felt the presence of Atticus all around him. A gentle breeze blew by rustling his hair. A smile came across Counticus' face and a soft laugh escaped him.

"Hello, Atticus." He smiled.

# Chapter 15

*It's time for me to show you the last of my memories.*
*So you can be equipped with the knowledge of what is to come*
*and understand the gift of foresight.*

Atticus' words ran warmly in his mind. After all the fighting Counticus' body felt at ease. The warmth of Atticus' presence embraced him with comfort and security. He was at peace as the images and memories poured in, as a soothing steady stream.

The image of Atticus appeared in his mind.

*Hi, Counticus.*
*I guess it might be weird to receive this message.*
*It might be even weirder since it's my memory.*

Atticus laughed at the notion.

*Sorry, not sorry? I guess . . . Anyway, it's time I left you with the last of my knowledge.*

The image of Atticus sitting on a stool, legs dangling and swaying back and forth appeared next.

*I was created by Lude and Farrin to be the means to an end for the nightmare. They had been trying to handle it for some time, but they couldn't finish it off. They made me as a third contender to help them. I was given the same abilities as them, just in case they should fall. At the very least they'd leave me behind to continue the work of saving Atticus. When we did battle with it, we didn't win. It got away. To that end I decided I would make you, Counticus. But rather than create you with the purpose of fulfilling my duties should I fail, I created you to be what is known as the Requiem persona. A vessel to house the other persona in case they should fall. Your job would be to keep their essences safe. The nightmare cannot open the door to the heart if all the keys are not present. The other persona are not as strong as Lude or Farrin, and they'll be easy pickings for the nightmare. But you? You'll be hard to track. You'll be hard to beat, and that will make for the perfect hiding place.*

*I've rambled a bit. I better cut this message here and I'll make another one.*

*See you soon!*

Atticus raised his hand to wave goodbye as the memory faded.

Soon another memory began. It showed Atticus walking by the lake in the valley.

*Hi again! I don't know about you, but I love it down here.*

He motioned to the lake. He stopped and turned to face the water for a moment. Taking a deep breath of the cool summer air, he could hear the sounds of bugs chirping all around.

*It's weird to think this place became such a trigger of pain in Atticus . . . he used to love coming here so much.*

He remained silent for a moment longer before shrugging and letting out a sigh. Then he continued his walk around the lake.

*I know you've heard us talk about this ability before, but Atticus was gifted by the goddess with a divine ability called foresight. It allows him to "know" what's coming. Don't confuse it with truesight though. Atticus can't see the future; he just feels it. But us persona? While we can't let his eyes or mind see the future, we persona do get to see it. Then we have to send those messages in the form of a 'gut feeling'. It's how we translate the images of the future back to his senses. Those are the rules of foresight.*

*Confusing, right? Deities are weird.*
*Anyways, thought you'd want to know.*
*I'll see you in the next one.*

He waved goodbye again and rotated his body to look out at the lake. He sat down in the tall grass, which now towered over him.

*I'm going to miss this place.*

He jolted his back straight and looked over his shoulder back at Counticus.

*Oops, I forgot to turn this thing off!*

He gave a playful sneer towards Counticus and stuck his tongue at him ending the memory.

Another memory played. This time he was in the woods walking up to an old cabin.

*Come on!*

He called in welcoming as he opened the doors to the wooden cabin. It was the cabin they appeared in when fleeing the nightmare.

*I'm sure you recognize this place. We escaped the nightmare and I brought you here. You're now probably wondering how I could know that if this is a recorded memory from the past right?*

He giggled covering his mouth as he pulled out a chair at the table. Looking at Counticus, he pointed to the side of his forehead.

*Foresight, remember? I've looked really far into the future, and I know you'll be seeing this message after I've made myself the final seal. I was really hoping the events would play out differently so we could protect Atticus together, but . . . well, it is what it is. Not all futures can be changed.*

He fidgeted in his seat a little. Sadness slipped across the boy's face. Atticus sniffled as he held back the tears.

*Anyway, I wanted you to know that someday another little boy will come here!*

*Not like you or me. He won't be a persona. He will be another child chosen by the goddess just like Atticus. I don't know his name though. It was really difficult to look that far ahead. It took me a lot of tries and a lot of effort to see that far into the future. It'll be a long long time until he gets here. Atticus is going to need you to keep fighting for him, okay? Fight for all of us, and don't give up hope! Someday the other boy will come, and he will be the final key you need in order to eradicate the nightmare for good. It's selfish to ask but . . . keep fighting the nightmare until he arrives. Okay?*

Atticus stared at the table with the expression of regret across his face. He looked up and opened his mouth to say more, but his eyes trailed back down the table and he shook his head. He looked up and gave a sad smile before the memory faded.

Another memory started. This time it showed Atticus looked out over a field of flowers that rolled down towards a lake. It's the valley again.

Atticus sat atop a log hunched over just looking down at the lake. He sat silently for a long time.

*I'm sorry, you know?*

*Sorry, that you have to do all this alone . . . it's not fair.*

*I know . . .*

*I wish we could be by your side in the events to come. But, we all had our roles to play. We did our best. I know you know that. I know you don't hold it against us. Still I wish things were different.*

*This is the last memory I have. Once you've watched it, you'll know how to use foresight yourself. Maybe as you get closer to the day the boy will arrive you can learn his name and even what he looks like. It was too far for me to see. I've tried a few more times, but no luck. Sorry about that but I can't take the ability any further, but I bet you could. You're the requiem persona! With all the powers of the others with you I'm sure you'll be able to do more with it than I could.*

The boy looked down with sadness in his eyes. His body hunched over as if the weight of the world rested upon his shoulders.

*I'm sorry we couldn't beat him without you . . . or with you . . . I saw you strike the final blows. That 'x' slash thing, that was amazing!*

He looked up a little bit.

*This was just too big for all of us. I'll keep the heart safe. I'll be the final seal and I won't budge for anyone but you, okay? Keep that necklace safe.*

He looked over at Counticus and gave a smile again.

*I know you can do it. So, stay strong, and know that even in the worst of times, you're not alone. Not really. We're all here with you, in here, and h ere.*

He gestured to the necklace Counticus wore and his chest.

*Good luck, Counticus.*

*I believe in you.*

*Goodbye.*

The boy smiled at Counticus as the memory faded.

The warmth of the place disappeared and the comforting embrace that surrounded Counticus was no more. When he opened his eyes, he stood before the stone door that lead to the heart of Atticus. The eyes that once glowed white were now shut, the face had returned to sleep.

He placed his hand against the stone door and looked up at the sleeping face.

"Good-bye my friend, sleep well. I'll see you soon."

Counticus backed away from the door, put his cupped hands together and the orbs on his bracelets lit up as he sang. The door sunk down into the depths once more and vanished from sight. He turned and walked back down the stone path. The cobblestones behind him returned to the depths as he walked away.

༄

—Some time later—

Counticus slouched in his seat in front of the control panel. The throne was simple in design, but its back towered over him. Wearing a blank t-shirt and loose fitting dark pants, his chin resting on his right wrist, fingers pressed into his cheek. He watched the wall across the room, seeing the world as the true Atticus sees it. Keeping watch to ensure the nightmare doesn't take control.

*It's been 10 years since Atticus became the final seal.*

*I've wrestled with that nightmare countless times. Keeping it away from Atticus.*

Memories of the battles revolve around the room. He dully looked at each as they pass by.

In most of the encounters he used the blades gifted to him by Farrin and Lude.

A memory of the nightmare standing over him.

*Almost lost it in that one.* He groaned.

Another scrolled by, showing him fighting three nightmares.

*Oh right, he learned how to copy himself that time. He was a lot weaker though.* He rolled his eyes remembering the encounter.

He switched to his opposite hand in his chair and adjusted his body accordingly.

*10 lonely years I have had to keep watch. I wished the others could be here. That's selfish I know. They did their best. They gave themselves to the cause. I'd be lying if I said it wasn't hard being here alone. I don't feel their warmth much these days . . . But the time is getting closer.*

He sat up and dug his elbows into his knees as he leaned forward to examine what the true Atticus saw.

His blue eyes shifted to a bright green.

*I've used foresight, you know. I've seen it.*

Images of what he had seen started to flicker like a scrapbook on the dark walls around him.

*The day is almost here when that boy will come. The savior of Atticus' soul.*

The images on the wall flip wildly from scene to scene. Some depicting a group of friends laughing, some of them arguing. Battles . . . so many battles. A dark lord, castles, beast-kin, magic, and so much more. When finally, an image paused on the wall of a young boy smiling and beside him a green translucent sphere creature. *It's a slime.*

*I know the day is coming when the goddess' chosen child will come.*

His eyes returned to blue and the images remained on the wall.

*I'll be here to greet you. My mission will soon come to an end, child of Sophia. The boy who is destined to save the world . . . .*

He leaned back in his chair deep in thought, as he watched the screen. His fingers strumming against his cheek as a smirk stretched across his face.

**To be Continued in A Kid and His Slime Series**

# Epilogue

It's been 10 years since I walked away from the merchant family. I still regret leaving them behind that day . . . but it felt right. I was in a place where I didn't think I could control myself anymore. A place where I struggled every day. Not knowing why, I did what I did, or why I felt how I felt. It's one of the worst feelings I've ever experienced.

It's weird when you feel like you are your own enemy. When you are warring with yourself. Lost to who you are and what you thought you should be.

I still can't believe all the blood I've shed in my life

There is no excuse for it really. But . . . I need to move forward. I can't keep hating myself for the mistakes of the past.

I've heard they're doing well though. I have thought about stopping by a few times but, it is probably better if I don't. They probably wouldn't recognize me now anyhow.

It's been a lonely road. Moving from place to place, never staying anywhere too long. Never having relationships with anyone. It's exhausting not being able to trust anyone. If only it was that simple to just confide in someone, to let my guard down, to rest. But . . . I can't. I continue to do my mercenary work, but sometime ago something in me changed. I didn't feel lost anymore. I finally found a purpose.

A reason to be. I don't hear those dark thoughts these days either. I finally feel free again.

A long time ago a voice reached out to me when I was at my lowest point, and I gave in to those desires. I turned into someone . . . something I never wanted to be. I let that rage rip through me and change who I was. I'm going to find who it was that spoke to me and get my answers. I need to know why.

Why me?

Why did you speak to me? Why did you fill my heart with such hatred?

Once I get my answer, I'll get my revenge. I'll put an end to them, so they never speak to anyone again. No one should ever be made to feel what I've felt. How many countless others have fallen to these whispers, these siren calls? I'm well on my way too. I've made 'friends' with a couple of these *lords of darkness*.

I caught wind recently that *he* has turned over a *new leaf*.

The Hero of Sophia. A young boy if you could believe it. Supposedly chosen by the goddess . . . just like me, and *him*. Only he used his gift to help the people of his kingdom. The big bad Dark Lord that has wrought nightmare for ages in that kingdom was defeated! By some 10-year-old kid and a group of misfits at that.

Not that I'm mad, it's great they've achieved so much. They actually used their gifts for doing what is right. But I heard an interesting rumor that said the Dark Lord has changed his ways and is now part of the boy's entourage.

Hmph. We'll see.

I know how easy it is to pretend to change. To start a new life, to *be different*. That darkness never leaves, even now I can sometimes feel those nightmarish thoughts rolling through me, griping me, choking me trying to break free. Thankfully they've mostly subsided. But I knew you before you changed into the *Dark Lord*. I remember when you were a prince. A leader for the people of Cawmmerce. I won't soon forget what you did that day.

I still remember the day you brought chaos and destruction to our home. You destroyed the Kingdom of Cawmmerce. I was there, and that was the day I lost my family. The day they were finally able to abandon me. I saw the monster you became. I saw you let the nightmare in.

So, I'm coming for you, your *majesty*, and you'll answer for your sins.

Atticus slammed the blade of his scythe into the dirt beside him. Looking off in the distance towards a group of people. One girl, one bearded man, a little boy, a slime, and a shadowy anthropomorphic dark bird.

# Prologue

**Diary Entry xx-xx-xx**

I can't believe it.

Someone knows them and where they live.

I'm anxious, and I'm scared. But, I must face them. I have to know why. Why they never found me, why they never looked. Did they mean to leave me, or did their efforts just yield no results? I'll go to them and ask them. I will ask them straight on *why did you never find me*?

I had been asking around in between jobs and pubs trying to locate my parents. I don't know why suddenly after all this time it's important to me . . . but it is. I've slipped coin and asked shopkeepers left and right. *Have you seen this man? Have you seen this woman?* And finally, one of my scouts gets back to me and points me in the direction of a small town.

I had to slip the woman a few coins to share the details with me, but when I also mentioned I was their long-lost son the guilt seemed to retreat from her eyes. She told me where they live, what they do, and how long they've been here. I am going to do it. I am going to get the answers from my parents on what happened that fateful day. The day our home was destroyed, and they fled without me, despite looking right in my direction.

*Memories of that day flooded back into my mind. My little hand reaching out to them crying out for them.*

*"Mommy!"*

*"Daddy!"*

*"Please wait, don't go without me. I'm here, I'm right here! Don't you see me, Mommy? Mommy? Mommy!"*

*I cried as I watched them turn and run with the others, fleeing the attack on our home. Why didn't she come for me? Did she really not see me or hear me? She looked right at me . . . she looked at me begging for her . . . why didn't you come, Mother?*

It was a five day walk by foot but finally out in the middle of nowhere I found their little hut. It was a small shack really, hardly something someone would call a house. There was a small plot of land that had various vegetables growing. Some strung up on sticks for the vines, others growing straight from the ground. A small shed nearby that I'm sure housed tools and supplies for the area. Near the garden sat empty rucksacks, buckets, a hoe, a scythe, and other tools readily available for a gardener.

⌘

He took a deep breath, heart pounding in his throat, sweat beading and dripping down his face. Atticus' palms were sweaty in his gloves, but he took another deep breath and mustered the courage to raise his hand and knock on the door. Four times his knuckles rapped.

It was an eternity of silence, but finally a lock turned, and the door creaked open. A startled face peered through the crack of the door.

"Hello? Who is it?" the voice asked. It was the gentle, but scared voice of a woman.

Atticus held his hand up and gave a soft smile.

"Hello, my name is . . . " but his sentence was cut off as the door opened.

The worn and tired face of the woman was easy to see now that the light shined upon it.

"You're . . . " she started, her voice cracking. She fidgeted with her hands, clenching her dress as she examined.

" . . . Atticus? Are you not?"

He nodded. His heart pounding like a boulder running down a hill, his mouth had suddenly got dry.

"My little boy has . . . come . . . home?" She fought back tears.

Tears streamed down his face. He felt embarrassed and scared but blurted out. "Hi Mom . . . " and she pushed herself through the doorway to embrace him crying out in surprise, tears of joy set free.

She held him tight, squeezing his shoulders, looking at his face, kissing his cheeks and embracing him again.

"Oh, my love. Look at the man you've grown into." She studied him in between showering him with affection.

He sat there smiling, speechless, his cheeks red, not knowing what to say.

*She sees me. She is here. Look at this greeting. She did want me. She didn't mean to leave me behind. I knew it. It was just a misunderstanding, decades of not knowing, poisoning the memory.*

"Well, come in, come in! You must be hungry!" She finally released him, brushing the dust away from her dress and took him by the hand dragging him inside the house.

"We don't have much, but I'll fix you something. Do you like tea, dear?" she asked, scurrying around the kitchen. He gave a nod and grunt which was enough for her to accept as a yes and she took straight to work. She brought over bread and jam, and hot tea. She wanted to be caught up on everything that happened to the boy. Never taking her eyes off him.

He told her everything there was to tell. About the day their home was attacked, how he tried calling out to them. How he searched for them. The days afterwards where he wandered from place to place. Escaping monsters, thugs, and thieves. How he spent much of his life on his own in the wild. The people he came across and how he eventually became a blade for hire. How he learned to master multiple weapon types and how it had saved his life on multiple occasions. He just spoke as things came to mind. The day was nearly done as dusk began to settle.

She gasped and oohed and awed at all the places as well. Completely enthralled with the tales he told her.

"Moth . . . Mom, hey, uh . . . I want to ask you something." he said anxiously as he fidgeted with his hands, thumbs twirling over one another. *I'm so nervous I can't even get my words straight between calling her Mom, like I did as a boy. Or formally as Mother since we've been estranged for so long. Get it together, Atticus!* He shook his head after his mental scolding.

"Sure, honey. What is it?" She smiled.

"Did . . . you ever come looking for me?" he finally blurted out.

She did not reply. Her expression faded and she looked down at her hands, clenching her dress.

"Mother, are you alright?" Atticus asked, seeing his mother's pain, and changing expression as she appeared lost in her own thoughts.

"Oh yes, dear, sorry. An unpleasant memory popped into my head. Sorry dear. What was it you wanted to ask?" Her voice staggered, cracking with a low reply, before being cleared and returning to her sweet sound.

He swallowed hard.

"Did you . . . ever . . . look for me? Did you ever try to find me? Did you see me that day when I reached out to you begging for you?" He turned his eyes down at his hands again.

Her eyes swelled up with tears as the memories of that day came over her. Before she could answer him, the door swung open and a bald, hunched over man slunk in. He was a tall and slender man. His skin was cracked and worn from the sun. It held his features tightly, as if his skin was at capacity holding the man's shape. The smell of booze and dirt filling the room.

"Who the 'ell are you?" the angry man pointed, growling at Atticus.

Atticus' eyes opened wide.

*I remember this. I remember him.* Memories of his father flashed before his eyes.

He remembered his dad always yelling, always working, and when he was home, he'd just yell at everyone for everything.

*"Can't you do anyfin' right?"*

*"You're a freak that's wot you are!"*

*"Knowing wot's to come but ye cannae do anythin' wit' it! A joke is wot you are. A mistake!"*

His father hated that he was *blessed* by the goddess. Since he couldn't use his ability to make his father any money, he thought him a freak and a monster.

"Wait a minute. I remember those pathetic lookin' eyes. How in the 'ell did you make it this long eh?" he barked at Atticus. "How the 'ell did you find us, eh?"

"That's enough!" His mother slammed her hands against the wooden table, the cups rattled and tea spilt from them soaking into the wood. She stood from her chair glaring at the man dead in his eyes.

"You will not speak to my son that way!" she yelled. She moved quickly for someone who looked so worn down. She pushed hard against the man's chest, and he stumbled back from each blow.

She had never had this much courage or strength to stand up to her husband. Seeing her boy home again had instilled a new strength in her. She was resolved to not lose him again. She wouldn't sit idly by anymore. This time, she would be there for her son.

"You will get out of my house until you sober up!" she ordered, giving him one last powerful shove. It caused him to trip over the door frame, his shoulders falling into the door, knocking it open, and his back landed against the dirt, his head smacking the ground where he fell unconscious. She proceeded to kick his legs out of the way of the door and shut it firmly, applying the lock once more.

"Mother!" Atticus said in surprise, standing up from the table.

She brushed her hands together and pushed her misplaced hair back behind her ear.

"Sorry, dear, but I won't stand for such behavior any longer." She touched his face.

"I lost you once, and I won't be losing you again, my love." She gave him the smile he always longed for.

*Mom...* His breath was staggered and heavy, tears filled his eyes as he processed his mother's actions.

"Oh, but you look tired, dear. Come on, I'll fix you a place to rest your head."

She took him into the small bedroom in the back and fixed him a place to sleep. He placed his sword and shield down under the bed, took his shoes off, crawled into bed pulling the wool blankets close.

His mother gave him a kiss on the head, told him she loved him, and reminded him she'd see him in the morning.

He smiled and closed his eyes, the image of his mother standing over him smiling as he went to sleep.

*I found her. I really found her. And she really wanted me, she wants me now.*

*I can't believe she stood up to him like that.*

Memories of his early childhood swept into his dreaming mind. Remembering the times his father had called him a monster or a freak.

*It was always his plan to have me be left behind. To be forgotten. He always said those things, always insisted. But instead of dragging me out there to do it himself he always forced her to do it. As if I was her problem.*

*Coward.*

The image of his father entered his dream and before his father stood Atticus as a child. The hand of his father slamming hard against his face knocking him to the ground.

"You're a freak!"

"You stupid little fing!"

"Get away from me, monster!"

"'ow did I end up with such a disgrace for a son aye?"

"Take 'im to the lake and leave 'im there. Ain't no one goin' tuh be lookin' for 'im. Let the wolves take 'im."

The image of him striking his mother and her falling to her knees appeared.

*"Coward!"* the child screamed at him.

"Wot did you say, you little shit?"

"You're a coward!" young Atticus roared, a flash taking over the memory, and the image of child Atticus vanished. In its place Atticus appeared. The man he had grown into and become today, despite everything that had happened.

Hot, sweat rolled down his face.

*It's hot . . . it's too hot.* He jolted awake. As he sat up in bed the heat was overbearing. It invaded his space as the fires roared as the walls burned.

"Mother!" he called out, coughing, his lungs feeling an immense pressure as he wheezed for air. He tugged his shirt up, holding it over his mouth as he tried to stand. His head was dizzy, and he fell onto his hands and knees losing his grip on his shirt, the cold dirt in between his fingers as he made his way from his room to the kitchen crawling below the smoke.

"Mom!" he shouted again, another cough rocking out of his chest.

*Where is she?* His mind racing, running in every possible direction. *I can't lose her now.*

He finally made his way to the front door. He mustered what strength he could and pulled himself back on his feet. He pushed his way through the door stumbling through the doorway out into the yard. He looked back to see dark smoke billowing from the door. The entire cottage was ablaze. Looking around as he suffered through a few hard coughs, he saw the crops were broken and damaged. The shed's roof was overtaken by fire as well. The light from the fires lit up the entire yard despite the blanket of night. His feet began pivoting in place as he turned to see if anyone else had made it out of the cottage. The silhouette of a person stood many steps away. As Atticus approached, he found it was his drunk father.

"Dad?" he asked softly.

"I ain't you're fuckin' dad, you freak!" he bellowed out as he turned around pointing a bloody dagger at Atticus.

*What?* The sight took him by surprise as he saw the tip of the blade drip blood. He looked behind his father to see his mother's body lying on the ground, staring up at him, her hand shaking as she reached for him.

"Mom!" he shouted as he ran to her.

"I don't fink so!" his father growled, taking a swing at Atticus, but he was too drunk to stand, let alone fight, so he tripped over his own feet and crashed to the ground, his dagger falling out of his hands, semi buried by the loose dirt.

Moving past his father Atticus fell to his knees sliding through the dirt and taking his mother's hand in his.

"Mom . . . I'm here!" he called out, tears escaping his eyes and falling onto her face.

"It's okay . . . my love . . . " she said in between breaths, as she gripped his hands.

He shook his head crying. He sat on the ground and pulled his mother close, cradling her with one arm while the other held her hand.

"I'm glad . . . I . . ." a raspy cough interrupted her words.

" . . . got to. . . see . . . you . . . one last . . . time." her breath short, and coughs came with every pause. She gave a bloody smile to her son.

He cried while he squeezed her hand. Holding her so tightly while his gaze was focused on her. He held on hoping it would somehow prevent what was about to happen.

"It's okay, my son." She said, smiling warmly at him, gripping him as tightly as she could.

"It's okay, my sweet boy. It's okay." she repeated.

"It's okay . . . it's . . . o-kay . . . ." Her breath whispered once more as life slipped away. Her head dropped to the side, her body becoming heavy, hand still clenching his, her eyes staring at the ground, vacant. Devoid of the warm and beautiful light he was reintroduced to. Gone.

"No!" he screamed his body, hunching over his mother while he held her. Tears streaming down his face, he felt the heat from her face grow cooler with each passing moment.

"If only that stupid bitch would've listened to me," his father said as he started to rise, pointing a finger at Atticus.

"But no, she just 'ad to 'ave the freak back in 'er life, eh? 'I'll die before I let 'im go!' she said and so 'ere she is." His father's words slurred while mocking the dead woman.

Atticus placed his mother's hands gently onto her chest and closed her eyes as he laid her softly on the ground. He placed a gentle kiss on her forehead, letting his cheek rest against hers, the last of her warmth fading away. He rose to his feet and turned to look at his father. Anger ripped through his expression as his final tears fell.

*That bastard. I'll kill you!* His mind raged. But, his heart told him to stop. He was frozen in place, not knowing what to do. When suddenly he heard a voice, a distant far away voice, reaching into his mind.

*Do it, Atticus.*
*Kill him.*
*Kill your father.*

He shook his head trying to free his mind.

*Listen to me.*
*He took everything away from you.*
*Your life.*
*Your family.*
*Your childhood.*
*Your future.*

Images flashed and snapped before Atticus as he was reminded of everything that happened.

*Your mother.*

His head jerked side to side as each memory came to remind him of all the pain his father had caused them. All the pain he had caused her.

*He deserves this.*
*Kill him and avenge your mother.*

His father drunkenly approached, staggering over his own feet as he pursued Atticus.

"I'll free meself of you, too!" His father slurred as he spoke.

*KILL HIM!*

*DO IT!*

❧

Lude let out a scream of pain.

"Farrin do something!" he cried out, his body convulsing. He gripped his chest trying to ease the pain.

"What is happening to you?" Farrin asked, hands open trying to help but not knowing what to do as he looked him up and down.

"I . . . don't know! It feels like something is tearing me apart, dude! Like . . . ahh!" He tried to explain but the pain was overpowering, and a scream of horror rushed from his throat. From his chest broke free a dark hand and then another. It placed its hands against Lude's chest and the creature began lifting itself out of Lude's body. As it pulled the rest of itself free Lude fell back and onto the floor. The figure stood staring at the two, it's eyes pulsed blood red, and its grin stretched from ear to ear.

"What the fuck is that?" Lude yelled. Wincing from the pain as he looked at the creature.

"Goddess help us . . . " Farrin muttered in a stunned state.

The figure jumped to the control panel.

Farrin helped Lude to his feet and the two rushed to the control panel to try and stop it.

༄

Memories of the past, and present flashed in Atticus' head as he struggled with his decision.

*DO IT!*

The voice screamed again. Atticus' head jerked back, and then slumped down to the ground. The images, memories, snapped into his mind over and over again. His mind made an audible snap as each memory slammed before him. Atticus opened his eyes as his father approached. His father paused in place now as he stared at Atticus.

"wot the 'ell?" the man questioned, noticing something had changed in Atticus.

Atticus stared hard back at his father. His eyes pulsed red, as red as blood, and he pushed past his drunk father, knocking him to the ground.

He headed inside the house to grab his sword, but as he walked through the doorway he paused. Snapping his neck to the side he walked backwards out of the door again, tilting his head the right to confirm what he saw. There it was, plain as day. A long black scythe.

*PERFECT.* He reached out grasping it in his hand.

"A SCYTHE. THAT COULD BE FUN," he joked spinning the scythe in his hands watching the light of the fire and moon gleam off the spinning blade.

He turned around and approached his father, brandishing the tip of the blade under his chin. His father dropped the dagger as the tip of the scythe blade dug into his chin. He winced at the pain, and looked up at his son as blood came from the broken skin

The sight caused Atticus to falter. He flinched and closed his eyes, fighting against the torrent of feelings swirling around in his chest.

༄

The two struggled to remove the nightmare from the control panel.

"Let go!" Farrin shouted, pulling on its left arm.

"Seriously!" Lude demanded, tugging on the right.

NO.

It smashed its arms together, knocking the two into each other. The two released its arms and collapsed on the floor. It then grabbed each one by the collars of their shirts and threw them far from the control panel. The pair plunged into the depths below and out of sight of the control panel.

∞

He shook his head, resolved once more to the cause, his eyes glowed red with ambition.

"Any last words?" he asked his father.

He apologized and begged for his life, and his eyes started to water. A low, groaned laugh that grew louder and louder to point of being deafening, even as the fire's roar filled the air.

"Actually, I don't care." he said coldly as he slammed the tip of the scythe into his father's chest. The blade plunged into the man, blood momentarily escaping out as the metal slammed into him. The scythe's blade lodged deep enough that it arched out from his back. Blood dripped down the curved blade and slowly ran from the chest wound.

He looked back at the house as it continued to burn. The weight of his father's body anchoring him. Focusing his grip, he ripped the scythe out of his father's chest, throwing him hard into the ground, sprawled out on his stomach in the dirt. Blood rushed into the ground from the gaping holes left by Atticus' assault. Atticus laid the scythe over his shoulder and rested his forearms over it. The fire's light danced upon the remaining blood that stained the blade. His father's face grew paler as the fire roared on, unaffected by the massacre. The only thing that could be heard was the roar of the fire and the forced breaths from his dying father. He turned his eyes toward Atticus, both shaking as he struggled to crane his gaze upwards. Coughing hoarsely, he spit blood from his mouth.

"I . . . always knew . . . you were . . . a monster . . . " His father's voice strained as he groaned out his final words.

Atticus turned his head just enough to look at his father from the side of his eye. The lack of light in this direction left this part of his face in darkness, but his bright pulsing red eyes stared hard into his father's. A smile stretched across his face, letting out a loud maniacal laugh and his father's head dropped into the ground as his last breath escaped his lungs.

# AFTERWORD

Why did I write this?

In case you found yourself wondering "why did he write a story like this?" then look no further!

A little back story. I used to write as a kid and eventually gave up in college. I returned to writing about 3 years ago, at 30, and started working on a novel called "A Kid and His Slime". Which is a story about a 10-year-old boy fated to save the world. I wrote about 24 chapters at around 45,000 words and then hit a roadblock. It took me about a year to write that. I ended up stuck and was struggling with narration style. The entire book had been written in third person, but I kept finding myself wanting to slip into first person with it. During that time, I had drafted up ideas for companion stories I wanted to tell for a couple characters that would appear in the 2 nd book. One was for a character named "Prince Phillip" and the other for a character named "Atticus". During hiatus I was really fighting myself and the project. As a way to try and tackle my own imposter syndrome I decided I'd write a companion story for Atticus first.

The goal was to make it a short story and be no more than 20,000 worlds. I was trying to set a realistic goal and I wanted to prove to myself I could finish it. Well, 45,000 words and about 8 months later I finally finished Atticus. Add in five more months for edits, re-reads, an editor, corrections, and etc. and we've come full circle. It took me about 13 months to completely finish Atticus, but here we are.

When I write, I typically pick a theme and try to write my project around that. For Atticus the theme was "inner war". I wanted to explore the effects we have on ourselves and how the external actions of others can impact us. I wanted to reflect the inner challenge we can face when we are fighting with who we are based off the events of the past. This turned out to be an incredible difficult project to complete.

Every step I took deeper into writing Atticus, the deeper I stepped into my own heart. I stepped back into events from my childhood. How certain things made me feel as a teenager and young adult. I looked back to video games and reflected on how some of those big scenes made me feel and what lasting impressions they left on me. Between all those things I mixed together the story for Atticus.

The closer I got to the end of finishing Atticus the louder and harder my own struggles internally became. I was warring with myself daily. Imposter syndrome was at an all time high. I kept fighting with notions that I wasn't good enough, I'm not really a writer, I can't finish this, no one will care, and other such thoughts. They really swallowed me up most days. I finally mustered the strength to finish. I remember being invigorated writing chapter 11-14, which in the 1 st draft was just chapter 11. When I finished, I said to myself "its now or never!" Knowing that if I didn't finish today, I might never come back and so I wrote chapter 11-15, the epilogue, and the prologue, all in one day. It was an incredible feeling to know that those inner thoughts we finally laid to rest as I crossed the finish line. Of course, they returned during the editing phase, but again here we are, across more finish lines.

This project became an extremely personal one and it meant a whole lot to me that I actually finished it.

So, in the end this project was made for folks who feel like me, and, for myself.

# UPCOMING PROJECTS

THEODIN.EXE

A Kid and His Slime

# ABOUT AUTHOR

What's good book reading fam!? I know my wife is out there cringing as she read that, but hey, that's how I like to introduce all my stuff.

My name is Charles Edwin, but most people call me Chuck. I was born and raised in Minnesota. I'm married to the most amazing person anyone could ask for and feel so blessed to have her with me. I also have three amazing children who bring so much joy into my life. I love all you goofy kids!

I love reading, making coffee, world building, and taking in the sights. But my biggest passion? You probably guessed it, video games! Growing up I spent a lot of time playing story and adventure games.

From Final Fantasy to the Legend of Zelda, these games became my life blood. They helped shape my opinions about life, what's right and wrong. They had me asking big questions about life. Brought me to and taught me humanity and humility. A few of my favorite story games are Final Fantasy, Xenoblade, The World Ends with You, and Mother 3. Honorable mentions: Fire Emblem and Dragon Quest.

As a kid I was often made to realize I didn't fit in with people. I did a lot of masking to avoid being alone. But despite that I always found myself at war with who I want to be vs who everyone else wanted me to be. As an adult I advocate for more open communication around mental health, self-love, and uplifting others. Doing whatever makes you happy and learning who you really are. I hope my stories can help there.

When I'm not writing I'm spending time with my amazing family. However, I often get lost in thought as I daydream about new stories or expanding current ones. The slightest stuff sends my mind into another dimension sometimes. I once daydreamed an entire story about breakfast food and my wife still encourages me to write that down. Maybe one day!

# Social Media

Instagram : Charlesedwinbooks

Tiktok : Chukkaq

Twitch: www.twitch.tv/chukkaq

Website : www.charlesedwinbooks.com

Patreon : www.patreon.com/charlesedwinbooks

On Instagram I post a lot about things that inspire me. Or about themes for a new projects, songs, etc. I also share sneak peaks about upcoming projects and reactions to game. Did I mentione I write game reviews in my free time?

Tiktok is more like a mini vlog. I talk about everything there. Kids, video games, games I'm playing now, streaming, books, its super random. It's all about stuff I like or that is relevant to me though.

On Twitch I play a lot of Breath of the Wild. I also take requests for story play throughs of JRPGs such as Final Fantasy, Xenoblade, and etc. I also love my cozy games and am an avid fan! My stream schedule is up on twitch so check it out for the latest up to date information!

My website is a great place to check out my personal blog, read game reviews, and get sneak peaks of upcoming projects!

Patreon is the place that hears everything first. If I have new projects in the works, announcements, covers, etc patreon is the very first place I post about it. If you find yourself into my stuff I'd recommend checking it out!

Made in United States
North Haven, CT
22 March 2023